Théophile Gautier's
Short Stories

THÉOPHILE GAUTIER
From a copper print

Théophile Gautier's
Short Stories

The Fleece of Gold
The Dead Leman
Poems, Etc.

Translated by
George Burnham Ives

With an Introduction by
Frédéric-César De Sumichrast

Short Story Index Reprint Series

BOOKS FOR LIBRARIES PRESS
FREEPORT, NEW YORK

First Published 1903
Reprinted 1970

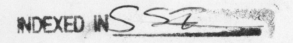
STANDARD BOOK NUMBER:
8369-3543-8

LIBRARY OF CONGRESS CATALOG CARD NUMBER:
73-122710

PRINTED IN THE UNITED STATES OF AMERICA

Contents

		PAGE
Théophile Gautier.	. . . .	ix
Tales:		
The Fleece of Gold	. . .	3
Arria Marcella	. . . .	105
The Dead Leman	. . .	175
The Nest of Nightingales	. .	247
Poems:		
Love at Sea	. . . .	263
Ars Victrix	. . . .	265
The Cloud	. . . .	268
The Poet and the Crowd	. .	270
The Portal	. . . .	272
The Caravan	. . . .	280
The Marsh	. . . .	281
Earth and the Seasons	. .	284
The Yellow Stains	. . .	285
The Chimera	. . . .	288

[v]

Introduction

Théophile Gautier

(1811–1872)

IN the happy youth of Romanticism, Gautier, like many another enthusiast, madly worshipped those painters in whom the gift of colour oft outweighed the sense of form. He was an adorer of the most glowing palettes, and the Venetians on the one hand and Rubens on the other won his constant praise. It so happened that the Museum of the Louvre was well provided with masterpieces of the one and the other school, and there it was that Gautier made his first acquaintance with the beauty and splendour of colour which, it must be owned, was sadly lacking in the works of the school of David and his successors.

Then, though he was later on to become one of the most persistent globe-trotters that France has ever turned out, he had not begun to travel when he felt the fascination of Rubens. That charm he has described time and again in his various articles and books; it held him fast; it compelled him to a quest as important in his eyes, at that time, as that of Jason or Sir Galahad. So he started for Belgium in the belief that it was a land filled to overflowing with splendid creatures, golden-haired, blue-eyed, and voluptuously formed. "The notion," he says in his account of the trip, "came into my mind in the Louvre Museum, as I was walking through the Rubens Gallery. The sight of his handsome women, with full forms, of those lovely and healthy bodies, of those mountains of rosy flesh with their wealth of golden hair, filled me with the desire to compare them with their living prototypes. . . I was on my way to the North in quest of the fairhaired female."

On that trip the one and only Rubens he beheld was "a stout kitchen-wench, with huge hips and amazingly large breasts, who was quietly sweeping the gutter, never for an instant suspecting that she constituted a most authentic Rubens. This find aroused in me hopes that proved subsequently absolutely deceitful."

It was on this disappointing experience that Gautier built up the pretty tale of *The Fleece of Gold* (1839), in which the hero is, naturally enough, a painter in search of just the same rarity, and, like Gautier, finds one specimen only. To have made the heroine of the tale a mere blowsy kitchen-wench would not, however, have suited the author's temperament. Gautier above all things was an artist: a lover of the Beautiful in its most refined and most exquisite form: quite capable, therefore, of idealising the somewhat gross type he had come upon in Valenciennes into the ethereal and delicate maiden engaged in the congenial and appropriate occupation of making lace instead of sweeping the gutter. Beyond this, the real object of the story is to afford oppor-

Introduction

tunity for the writer to talk upon art, and Rubens in particular; to develop his views upon colour in painting, and to indulge his taste for the description of a quaint old place such as Antwerp had not altogether ceased to be. The love story is merely subordinate to this principal purpose, just as at times in Balzac's novels one wonders whether the conflict of human passions and greed has not been introduced merely as a sop to a reader whom the prolonged descriptions of things might otherwise repel.

The human element, indeed, in Gautier's tales is never very masterful. It is apparently indispensable to the satisfaction of the public, and writing for that unsatisfactory public, Gautier yields the point, but his heart is less in that part of the work than in the one which gives him scope for the exposition of his most cherished beliefs, and especially of his diatribes against civilisation and the unspeakable *bourgeois,* whom he abominated as heartily as did Flaubert. He consequently introduces

Introduction

some other element of interest: the search for what does not exist, or exists only in rare cases, as in *The Fleece of Gold;* the mysterious and fanciful, as in *The Dead Leman* (1836); the profound delight of music and its strange consequences, as in *The Nest of Nightingales* (1833), or picturesqueness, in some form or other, as in *Militona, The Quartette, Fortunio,* and many another tale and novel.

Nor is *Arria Marcella* (1852), the second story in this collection, any exception to the rule. At first glance it may appear to be a love tale, pure and simple, but it quickly becomes plain that the real delight Gautier takes in his subject is the evocation of a past that strikes him as far superior as an embodiment of Beauty to the utterly commonplace civilisation of the nineteenth century in which, he might almost say, it was his misfortune, as it was Célestin Nanteuil's, to be condemned to live.

Besides, it was the fashion, in those Romanticist times, to indulge in evocations of the past. The fashion had been set by Chateaubriand in his *Martyrs,* which inspired Augustin Thierry to become an historian and to delve into the archives of France. Flaubert, ere long, though a realist in the more important part of his work, followed the same path and gave to the public *Salammbô* and *Herodias.* Gautier, therefore, was merely pleasing the readers of his works and obeying a widespread impulse when he composed *Arria Marcella* and *The Romance of a Mummy,* recalling Pompeii in the one and ancient Egypt in the other.

There was, however, still another cause: the influence of Hoffmann, the author of fantastic tales, exceedingly popular in those days and by no means forgotten even now. Gautier studied Hoffmann to some purpose, and appreciated the skillful manner in which the German writer produced the impression of the strange and the mysterious by the use of absolutely legitimate means. "Hoffmann's use of the marvellous," he says in an article upon the *Tales,* "is not quite analogous to

Introduction

the use of it in fairy tales; he always keeps in touch with the world of reality, and rarely does one come across a palace of carbuncles with diamond turrets in his works, while he makes no use whatever of the wands and talismans of *The Thousand and One Nights*. The supernatural elements to which he commonly has recourse are occult sympathy and antipathy, curious forms of mania, visions, magnetism, and the mysterious and malignant influence of a vaguely indicated principle of evil. It is the positive and plausible side of the fantastic; and in truth Hoffmann's tales should be called tales of caprice or fancy rather than fantastic tales."

It is plainly Hoffmann's method that Gautier has adopted in the composition of *Arria Marcella*, and of *The Nest of Nightingales,* as also in *The Dead Leman.* The reader is puzzled to know whether the adventures of Octavian, the young priest, and the maidens twain are real or fanciful; whether the two former dreamed dreams or actually experienced the astounding delights, at once bewildering and hideous, which the novelist relates so seriously. This is where the story-teller's art plays its part to perfection.

The Nest of Nightingales, nevertheless, should not be classed with the other two tales of mystery or fancy. It is more an idealisation of music; an attempt to symbolise the genius of that art and the effect upon its devotees. It is one of the most exquisite tales Gautier ever wrote, and has ever remained deservedly popular. It exhibits all his grace, all his lightness of touch, all his deep sense of Beauty.

For, with him, it is always to Beauty, ideal, abstract Beauty, that one returns. Beauty was the one cult of his life; the deity to which he was never for an instant unfaithful. He believed in it; he strove after it; he endeavoured to make men feel it; he was roused to wrath by the incapacity of the greater number of his readers to conceive even what it really is, and many of his exaggerations in the Romanticist line are due simply to the irritation aroused in him by the dullness and slow-wittedness of the *profanum vulgus,* whom he despised as cordially as did Horace, and whom he detested even more than did the Roman singer.

In his verse, more especially, did he strive to attain that perfection of form which is the outer and visible symbol of the deeper, hidden glory that, living within his poet's heart, sang to him its melodious hymn.   Hence it is that his verse is well-nigh untranslatable and that an approach to its wondrous exquisiteness alone can be made.   At a time when the Romanticist doctrine of fullest liberty in art had logically entailed neglect of form, when loose riming and careless turns had become almost the rule among the less well-endowed poets, Gautier stood up for the principle that the matter itself is not sufficient unless it be clothed in the most perfect form of which it is susceptible.   This became the burden of his teaching; and the lines he wrote, no

Introduction

matter upon what subject, were intended
to illustrate this truth.   It led to the doctrine
of art for art's sake; and that, in its turn,
induced many a false conclusion, but not in
Gautier. If the matter he selected did not
always rank high, there never was, at least,
anything gross in his verse—even *Albertus*,
though undoubtedly sensual, cannot be called
gross.   And invariably the form was superb,
the language choice, the melody sure, the
rhythm admirable, the rime of the best.

His marvellous command of language, his
astonishingly rich vocabulary, and, in addition,
his deep sense of colour and harmony, aided
him in turning out the volume known as
Enamels and Cameos, in which he amassed
gems of verse.   He was above all other
writers of his day the one who most fully
comprehended colour and was best able to
communicate the sensation of it by the use of
words.   For him, as I have said elsewhere,
"words were not mere aggregations of
letters or syllables, having each and all a

definite meaning attached to them and nothing more. They were not simply a means, when assembled, of communicating ideas. They had qualities and properties of their own — intimately, essentially their own — which gave them a value wholly apart from any usefulness they might possess as replacing the primitive language of signs. They were full of colour, they were colour; they were full of music, they were music's self; they were sculpture and architecture; they were metal; and they were stuffs of richest loom—silk and satin, gauze and lawn, velvet and brocade; they were gems and stones of purest ray serene; they blazed with internal fires; they were refulgent with internal glow; they burned with dull flame and shone with scintillation resplendent. No precious metal, no pearl of finest orient but was to be found among them. Every shade and hue of colour, every sound and note of music was given out by them."

Hence it is exceedingly difficult to give in

any other tongue an adequate idea of Gautier's verse, since so much of its beauty depends not upon the matter of which he treats, but upon the form he has given it. And it is precisely this form which escapes the translator, or allows itself to be partially reproduced only. Yet not to include in a volume of selections from Gautier's varied work some examples of his versification would be to leave the volume incomplete, and the reader might well complain because Gautier the poet was unduly neglected in favour of Gautier the story-teller.

The Fleece of Gold

The Fleece of Gold

I

TIBURCE was really a most extraordinary young man; his oddity had the peculiar merit of being unaffected; he did not lay it aside on returning home, as he did his hat and gloves; he was original between four walls, without spectators, for himself alone.

Do not conclude, I beg, that Tiburce was ridiculous, that he had one of those aggressive manias which are intolerable to all the world; he did not eat spiders, he played on no instrument, nor did he read poetry to anybody. He was a staid, placid youth, talking little, listening less; and his half-opened eyes seemed to be turned inward.

He passed his life reclining in the corner of a divan, supported on either side by a pile of cushions, worrying as little about the affairs of the time as about what was taking place in the moon. There were very few substantives which had any effect on him, and no one was ever less susceptible to long words. He cared absolutely nothing for his political rights, and thought that the people were still free at the wine-shop.

His ideas on all subjects were very simple; he preferred to do nothing rather than to work; he preferred good wine to cheap wine and a beautiful woman to an ugly one; in natural history he made a classification than which nothing could be more succinct: things that eat, and things that do not eat. In brief, he was absolutely detached from all human affairs, and was as reasonable as he appeared mad.

He had not the slightest self-esteem; he did not deem himself the pivot of creation, and realised fully that the world could turn without his assistance; he thought little more of himself than of the rind of a cheese, or of the eels in vinegar. In face of eternity and the infinite, he had not the courage to be vain; having looked sometimes through the microscope and the telescope, he had not an exaggerated idea of the importance of the human race. His height was five feet, four inches; but he said to himself that the people in the sun might well be eight hundred leagues tall.

Such was our friend Tiburce.

It would be a mistake to think from all this that Tiburce was devoid of passions. Beneath the ashes of that placid exterior smouldered more than one burning brand. However, no one knew of any regular mistress of his, and he displayed little gallantry towards women. Like almost all the young men of to-day, without being precisely a poet or a painter, he had read many novels and seen many pictures; lazy as he was, he preferred to live on the faith of other people; he loved with the poet's love, he looked with the eyes of the artist, and he was familiar with more poets than faces; reality was repugnant to him, and by dint of living in books and paintings, he had reached the point where nature no longer rang true.

The Madonnas of Raphael, the courtesans of Titian, caused the most celebrated beauties to seem ugly to him; Petrarch's Laura, Dante's Beatrice, Byron's Haidee, André Chénier's Camille, threw completely into the shade the women in hats, gowns, and shoulder-capes whose lover he might have been. And yet he did not demand an ideal with white wings and a halo about her head; but his studies in antique statuary, the Italian schools, his familiarity with the masterpieces of art, and his reading of the poets had given him an exquisitely refined taste in the matter of form, and it would have been impossible for him to love the noblest mind on earth, unless it had the shoulders of the Venus of Milo. So it was that Tiburce was in love with no one.

His devotion to abstract beauty was manifested by the great number of statuettes, plaster casts, drawings and engravings with which his room and its walls were crowded, so that the ordinary bourgeois would have considered it rather an impossible abode; for he had no furniture save the divan mentioned above, and several cushions of different colours scattered over the carpet. Having no secrets, he could easily do without a secretary, and the incommodity of commodes was to him an established fact.

Tiburce rarely went into society, not from shyness, but from indifference; he welcomed his friends cordially, and never returned their visits. Was Tiburce happy? No; but he was not unhappy; he would have liked, however, to dress in red. Superficial persons accused him of insensibility, and kept women said that he had no heart; but in reality his was a heart of gold, and his search for physical beauty betrayed to observant eyes a painful disillusionment in the world of moral beauty. In default of sweetness of perfume, he sought grace in the vessel containing it; he did not complain, he indulged in no elegies, he did not wear ruffles *en pleureuse;*

but one could see that he had suffered, that he had been deceived, and that he proposed not to love again except with his eyes open. As dissimulation of the body is much more difficult than dissimulation of the mind, he set much store by material perfection; but alas! a lovely body is as rare as a lovely soul. Moreover, Tiburce, depraved by the reflections of novel-writers, living in the charming, imaginary society created by poets, with his eyes full of the masterpieces of statuary and painting, had a lordly and scornful taste; and that which he took for love was simply the admiration of an artist. He found faults of drawing in his mistress; although he did not suspect it, woman was to him a model, nothing more.

One day, having smoked his hookah, having gazed at Correggio's threefold Leda in its filleted frame, having turned Pradine's latest statuette about in every direction, having taken his left foot in his right hand and his right foot in his left hand, and having placed his heels on the edge of the mantel, Tiburce was forced to admit to himself that he had come to the end of his means of diversion, that he knew not which way to turn, and that the gray spiders of ennui were crawling down the walls of his room, all dusty with drowsiness.

He asked the time, and was told that it was a quarter to one, which seemed to him decisive and unanswerable. He bade his servant dress him and went out to walk the streets; as he walked he reflected that his heart was empty, and he felt the need of "making a passion," as they say in Parisian slang.

This laudable resolution formed, he propounded the following questions to himself: Shall I love a Spaniard with an amber complexion, frowning eyebrows, and jet-black hair? Or an Italian with classic features, and orange-tinted eyelids encircling a glance of flame? or a slim-waisted Frenchwoman, with a nose *à la* Roxelane and a doll's foot? or a red Jewess with a sky-blue skin and green eyes ? or a negress, black as night, and gleaming like new bronze ? Shall I have a fair or a dark passion ? Terrible perplexity.

As he plodded along, head down, pondering this question, he ran against something hard, which caused him to jump back with a blood-curdling oath. That something was a painter friend of his; together they entered the Museum. The painter, an enthusiastic admirer of Rubens, paused by preference before the canvases of the Dutch Michelangelo, whom he extolled with a most contagious frenzy of admiration. Tiburce, surfeited with the Greek outline, the Roman contour, the tawny tones of the Italian masters, took delight in the plump forms, the satiny flesh, the ruddy faces, as blooming as bouquets of flowers, the luxuriant health that the Antwerpian artist sends bounding through the veins of those faces of his, with their network of blue and scarlet. His eye caressed with sensuous pleasure those lovely pearl-white shoulders and those siren-like hips drowned in waves of golden hair and marine pearls. Tiburce, who had an extraordinary faculty of assimilation, and who understood equally well the most contrasted types, was at that moment as Flemish as if he had been born in the *polders,* and had never lost sight of Lillo fort and the steeples of Antwerp.

"It is decided," he said to himself as he left the gallery, "I will love a Fleming."

As Tiburce was the most logical person in the world, he placed before himself this irrefutable argument, namely, that Flemish women must be more numerous in Flanders than elsewhere, and that it was important for him to go to Belgium at once — *to hunt the blonde.* This Jason of a new type, in quest of another fleece of gold, took the Brussels diligence that same evening, with the mad haste of a bankrupt weary of intercourse with men and feeling a craving to leave France, that classic home of the fine arts, of lovely women, and of sheriffs' officers.

After a few hours, Tiburce, not without a thrill of joy, saw the Belgian lion appear on the signs of inns, beneath a poodle in nankeen breeches, accompanied by the inevitable *Verkoopt men dranken*. On the following evening he walked on Magdalena Strass in Brussels, climbed the mountain with its kitchen gardens, admired the stained-glass windows of St. Gudule's and the belfry of the Hôtel de Ville, and scrutinised, not without alarm, all the women who passed.

He met an incalculable number of negresses, mulattresses, quadroons, half-breeds, griffs, yellow women, copper-coloured women, green women, women of the colour of a boot-flap, but not a single blonde; if it had been a little warmer, he might have imagined himself at Seville; nothing was lacking, not even the black mantilla.

As he returned to his hotel on Rue d'Or, however, he saw a girl who was only a dark chestnut, but she was ugly. The next day he saw, near the *residenz* of Laeken, an Eng-

lishwoman with carroty-red hair and light-
green shoes; but she was as thin as a frog
that has been shut up in a bottle for six
months, to act as a barometer, which ren-
dered her inapt to realise an ideal after the
style of Rubens.

Finding that Brussels was peopled solely
by Andalusians with *burnished breasts,* —
which fact is readily explained by the Spanish
domination that held the Low Countries in
subjection so long — Tiburce determined to
go to Antwerp, thinking, with some appearance of reason, that the types familiar to
Rubens and so constantly reproduced on his
canvases were likely to be frequently met
with in his beloved native city.

He betook himself, therefore, to the station
of the railway that runs from Brussels to Antwerp. The steam horse had already eaten
his ration of coal; he was snorting impatiently and blowing from his inflamed nostrils, with a strident noise, dense puffs of white
smoke, mingled with showers of sparks.

Tiburce seated himself in his compartment, in company with five Walloons, who sat as motionless in their places as canons in the chapter-house, and the train started. The pace was moderate at first; they moved little faster than one rides in a post-chaise at ten francs the relay; but soon the beast became excited and was seized with a most extra-ordinary rage for rapidity. The poplars beside the track fled to right and left like a routed army; the landscape became blurred and was blotted out in a gray vapour; the colewort and the peony studded the black strips of ground with indistinct stars of gold and azure. Here and there a slender spire appeared amid the billowing clouds and disappeared instantly, like the mast of a ship on a stormy sea. Tiny light-pink or apple-green wine-shops made a fleeting impression on the eye at the rear of their gardens, beneath their garlands of vines or hops; here and there pools of water, en-circled by dark mud, dazzled the eye like the mirror in a trap for larks. Meanwhile the iron monster belched forth with an ever-increasing roar its breath of boiling steam; it puffed like an asthmatic whale; a fiery sweat bathed its brazen sides. It seemed to complain of the insensate swiftness of its pace and to pray for mercy to its begrimed postillions, who spurred it on incessantly with shovelfuls of coal. There came a noise of bumping carriages and rattling chains: they had arrived.

Tiburce ran to right and left without fixed purpose, like a rabbit suddenly released from its cage. He took the first street that he saw, then a second, then a third, and plunged bravely into the heart of the ancient city, seeking the blonde with an ardour worthy of the knights-errant of old.

He saw a vast number of houses painted mouse-gray, canary-yellow, sea-green, pale lilac; with roofs like stairways, moulded gables, doors with vermiculated bosses, with short stout pillars, decorated with quadrangular bracelets like those at the Luxembourg, leaded Renaissance windows, gargoyles, carved beams, and a thousand curious architectural details, which would have enchanted him on any other occasion; he barely glanced at the illuminated Madonnas, at the Christs bearing lanterns at the street corners, at the saints of wax or wood with their gewgaws and tinsel — all those Catholic emblems that have so strange a look to an inhabitant of one of our Voltairean cities.   Another thought absorbed him: his eyes sought, through the dark, smoke-begrimed windows, some fairhaired feminine apparition, a tranquil and kindly Brabantine face, with the ruddy freshness of the peach, and smiling within its halo of golden hair.   He saw only old women making lace, reading prayer-books, or squatting in corners and watching for the passing of an infrequent pedestrian, reflected by the glass of their *espions,* or by the ball of polished steel hanging in the doorway.

The streets were deserted, and more silent than those of Venice; no sound was to be heard save that of the chimes of various churches striking the hours in every possible key, for at least twenty minutes. The pavements, surrounded by a fringe of weeds, like those in the courtyards of unoccupied houses, told of the infrequency and small number of the passers-by. Skimming the ground like stealthy swallows, a few women, wrapped discreetly in the folds of their dark hoods, glided noiselessly along the houses, sometimes followed by a small boy carrying their dog. Tiburce quickened his pace, in order to catch a glimpse of the features buried beneath the shadow of the hood, and saw there pale faces, with compressed lips, eyes surrounded by dark circles, prudent chins, delicate and circumspect noses — the genuine type of the pious Roman or the Spanish duenna; his burning glance was shattered against dead glances, the glassy stare of a dead fish.

From square to square, from street to street, Tiburce arrived at last at the Quay of the Scheldt by the Harbour Gate. The magnificent

spectacle extorted a cry of surprise from him;
an endless number of masts, yards, and cordage resembled a forest on the river, stripped
of leaves and reduced to the state of a mere
skeleton. The bowsprits and latteen yards
rested familiarly on the parapet of the wharf,
as a horse rests his head on the neck of his
carriage-mate. There were Dutch *orques,*
round-sterned, with their red sails; sharp,
black American brigs, with cordage as fine as
silk thread; salmon-coloured Norwegian koffs,
emitting a penetrating odour of planed fir;
barges, fishermen, Breton salt-vessels, English
coalers, ships from all parts of the world.
An indescribable odour of sour herring, to-
bacco, rancid suet, melted tar, heightened by
the acrid smells of the ships from Batavia,
loaded with pepper, cinnamon, ginger, and
cochineal, floated about in the air in dense
puffs, like the smoke from an enormous per-
fume-pan lighted in honour of commerce.

Tiburce, hoping to find the true Flemish
type among the lower classes, entered the

taverns and gin-shops. He drank lambick, white beer of Louvain, ale, porter, and whiskey, desiring to improve the opportunity to make the acquaintance of the northern Bacchus. He also smoked cigars of several brands, ate salmon, sauerkraut, yellow potatoes, rare roast-beef, and partook of all the delights of the country.

While he was dining, German women, chubby-faced, swarthy as gypsies, with short skirts and Alsatian caps, came to his table and squalled unmelodiously some dismal ballad, accompanying themselves on the violin and other unpleasant instruments. Blonde Germany, as if to mock at Tiburce, had besmeared itself with the deepest shade of sunburn; he tossed them angrily a handful of small coins, which procured him the favour of another ballad of gratitude, shriller and more uncivilised than the first.

In the evening he went to the music-halls to see the sailors dance with their mistresses; all of the latter had beautiful, glossy-black hair that shone like a crow's wing. A very pretty Creole seated herself beside him and familiarly touched her lips to his glass, according to the custom of the country, and tried to enter into conversation with him in excellent Spanish, for she was from Havana; she had such velvety-black eyes, a pale complexion, so warm and golden, such a small foot, and such a slender figure, that Tiburce, exasperated, sent her to all the devils, to the great surprise of the poor creature, who was little accustomed to such a greeting.

Utterly insensible to the dark perfections of the dancers, Tiburce withdrew to the Arms of Brabant Hotel. He undressed in a dissatisfied frame of mind, and wrapping himself as well as he could in the openwork napkins which take the place of sheets in Flanders, he soon slept the sleep of the just.

He had the loveliest dreams imaginable.

The nymphs and allegorical figures of the Medici Gallery, in the most enticing *déshabillé*, paid him a nocturnal visit; they gazed fondly at him with their great blue eyes, and smiled at him in the most friendly way, with their lips blooming like red flowers amid the milky whiteness of their round, plump faces. One of them, the Nereid in the picture called *The Queen's Voyage,* carried familiarity so far as to pass her pretty taper fingers, tinged with carmine, through the hair of the love-lorn sleeper. Drapery of flowered brocade cleverly concealed the deformity of her scaly legs, ending in a forked tail; her fair hair was adorned with seaweed and coral, as befits a daughter of the sea; she was adorable in that guise. Groups of chubby children, as red as roses, swam about in a luminous atmosphere, holding aloft wreaths of flowers of insupport-able brilliancy, and drew down from heaven a perfumed rain. At a sign from the Nereid, the nymphs stood in two rows and tied to-gether the ends of their long auburn hair, in such wise as to form a sort of hammock of gold filigree for the fortunate Tiburce and his finny mistress; they took their places therein, and the nymphs swung them to and fro, moving their heads slightly with a rhythm of infinite sweetness.

Suddenly there was a sharp noise, the golden threads broke, and Tiburce fell to the ground. He opened his eyes and saw naught save a horrible bronze-coloured face, which fastened upon him two great enamel eyes, only the whites of which could be seen.

"Your breakfast, *mein Herr,*" said an old Hottentot negress, a servant of the hotel, placing on a small table a salver laden with dishes and silverware.

"Damnation! I ought to have gone to Africa to look for blondes!" grumbled Tiburce, as he attacked his beefsteak in desperation.

II

TIBURCE, having duly satisfied his appetite, left the Arms of Brabant with the laudable and conscientious purpose of continuing the search for his ideal. He was no more fortunate than on the previous day; dark-skinned ironies, emerging from every street, cast sly and mocking glances at him; India, Africa, America passed before him in specimens more or less copper-coloured; one would have said that the venerable city, advised of his purpose, concealed in a spirit of mockery, in the depths of its most impenetrable back yards and behind its dingiest windows, all those of its daughters who might have recalled, vividly or remotely, the paintings of Jordaens or Rubens; stingy with its gold, it was lavish with its ebony.

Enraged by this sort of mute ridicule, Tiburce visited the museums and galleries, to escape it. The Flemish Olympus shone once more before his eyes. Once more cascades of hair glistened in tiny reddish waves, with a quiver of gold and radiance; the shoulders of the allegories, refurbishing their silvery whiteness, glowed more vividly than ever; the blue of the eyes became lighter, the ruddy cheeks bloomed like bunches of carnations; a pink vapour infused warmth into the bluish pallor of the knees, elbows, and fingers of all those fair-haired goddesses; soft gleams of changing light, ruddy reflections played over the plump, rounded flesh; the pigeon-breast draperies swelled before the breath of an invisible wind, and began to flutter about in the azure vapour; the fresh, plump Netherlandish poesy was revealed in all its entirety to our enthusiastic traveller.

But these beauties on canvas were not enough for him. He had come thither in search of real, living types. He had fed long enough on written and painted poetry, and he had discovered that intercourse with abstractions was somewhat unsubstantial. Doubtless it would have been much simpler to stay in Paris and fall in love with a pretty woman, or even with an ugly one, like everybody else; but Tiburce did not understand nature and was able to read it only in translations. He grasped admirably all the types realised in the works of the masters, but he would not have noticed them of his own motion if he had met them on the street or in society; in a word, if he had been a painter, he would have made vignettes based on the verses of poets; if he had been a poet, he would have written verses based on the pictures of painters. Art had taken possession of him when he was too young, and had corrupted him and prejudiced him. Such instances are more common than is supposed in our over-refined civilisation, where we come in contact with the works of man more often than with those of nature.

For a moment Tiburce had an idea of compromising with himself, and made this cowardly and ill-sounding remark: "Chestnut hair is a very pretty colour." He even went so far, the sycophant, the villain, the man of little faith, as to admit to himself that black eyes were very bright and very attractive. It may be said, to excuse him, that he had scoured in every direction, and without the slightest result, a city which everything justified him in believing to be radically blonde. A little discouragement was quite pardonable.

At the moment that he uttered this blasphemy under his breath, a lovely blue glance, wrapped in a mantilla, flashed before him and disappeared like a will-o'-the-wisp around the corner of Meïr Square.

Tiburce quickened his pace, but he saw nothing more; the street was deserted from end to end. Evidently the flying vision had entered one of the neighbouring houses, or had vanished in some unknown alley. Tiburce, bitterly disappointed, after glancing at the well, with the iron scrollwork forged by Quintin Metzys, the painter-locksmith, took it into his head to visit the cathedral, which he found daubed from top to bottom with a horrible canary-yellow. Luckily the wooden pulpit, carved by Verbruggen, with its decoration of foliage alive with birds, squirrels, and turkeys displaying their plumage, and all the zoölogical equipage which surrounded Adam and Eve in the terrestrial paradise, redeemed that general insipidity by the delicacy of its angles and its nicety of detail. Luckily, the blazonry of the noble families, and the pictures of Otto Venius, of Rubens, and of Van Dyck, partly concealed that hateful colour, so dear to the middle classes and to the clergy.

A number of Beguins at prayer were scattered about on the pavement of the church; but the fervour of their piety caused them to bend their faces so low over their red-edged prayer-books, that it was difficult to distinguish their features. Moreover, the sanctity of the spot and the venerable aspect of their costumes prevented Tiburce from feeling inclined to carry his investigation farther.

Five or six Englishmen, breathless after ascending and descending the four hundred and seventy stairs of the steeple, to which the dove's-nests with which it is always capped give the aspect of an Alpine peak, were examining the pictures, and, trusting only in part to their guide's loquacious learning, were hunting up in their guide-books the names of the masters, for fear of admiring one thing for another; and they repeated in front of every canvas, with imperturbable stolidity: " It is a very fine exhibition." These Englishmen had squarely-cut faces, and the enormous distance between their noses and their chins demonstrated the purity of the breed. As for the English lady who was with them, she was the same one whom Tiburce had previously seen at the *residenz* of Laeken; she wore the same green boots and the same red hair. Tiburce, despairing of finding Flemish blondes, was almost on the point of darting a killing glance at her; but the vaudeville coup-lets aimed at perfidious Albion came to his mind most opportunely.

In honour of these visitors, so manifestly Britannic, who could not move without a jingling of guineas, the beadle opened the shut-ters which, during three-fourths of the year, concealed the two wonderful paintings of the *Crucifixion* [1] and the *Descent from the Cross*.

---

[1] The painting entitled *Le Coup de Lance*.—[Ed.]

The Fleece of Gold

The *Crucifixion* is a work that stands by itself, and Rubens, when he painted it, was thinking of Michelangelo. The drawing is rough, savage, impetuous, like those of the Roman school; all the muscles stand out at once, all the bones and sinews are visible, nerves of steel are surrounded by flesh like granite. Here is no trace of the joyous, ruddy tones with which the Antwerpian artist nonchalantly sprinkles his innumerable productions; it is the Italian bistre in its tawniest intensity; executioners, colossi shaped like elephants, have tigers' muzzles and attitudes of bestial ferocity; even the Christ Himself, included in this exaggeration, wears rather the aspect of a Milo of Crotona, nailed to a wooden horse by rival athletes, than of a God voluntarily sacrificing Himself for the redemption of humanity. There is nothing Flemish in the picture save the great Snyders dog barking in a corner.

When the shutters of the *Descent from the Cross* were thrown open, Tiburce was dazzled and seized with vertigo, as if he had looked into an abyss of blinding light; the sublime head of the Magdalen blazed triumphantly in an ocean of gold, and seemed to illuminate with the beams from its eyes the pale, gray atmosphere that filtered through the narrow Gothic windows. Everything about him faded away; there was an absolute void; the square-jawed Englishman, the red-haired Englishwoman, the violet-robed beadle —he saw them no more.

The sight of that face was to Tiburce a revelation from on high; scales fell from his eyes, he found himself face to face with his secret dream, with his unavowed hope; the intangible image which he had pursued with all the ardour of an amorous imagination, and of which he had been able to espy only the profile or the ravishing fold of a dress; the capricious and untamed chimera, always ready to unfold its restless wings, was there before him, fleeing no more, motionless in the splendour of its beauty. The great master had copied in his own heart the anticipated and longed-for mistress; it seemed to him that he himself had painted the picture; the hand of genius had drawn unerringly and with broad strokes of the brush what was only confusedly sketched in his mind, and had garbed in gorgeous colours his undefined fancy for the unknown. He recognised that face, and yet he had never seen it.

He stood there, mute, absorbed, as insensible as a man in a cataleptic fit, not moving an eyelid and plunging his eyes into the boundless glance of the great penitent.

A foot of the Christ, white with a bloodless whiteness, as pure and lifeless as a consecrated wafer, hovered with all the inert listlessness of death over the saint's white shoulder, an ivory footstool placed there by the sublime artist to enable the divine corpse to descend from the tree of redemption. Tiburce felt jealous of the Christ. For such a blessed privilege he would gladly have endured the Passion. The bluish pallor of the flesh

hardly reassured him. He was deeply
wounded, too, because the Magdalen did
not turn towards him her melting, glistening
eye, wherein the light bestowed its diamonds
and grief its pearls. The dolorous and impassioned persistence of that glance, which
wrapped the beloved body in a winding-
sheet of love, seemed to him humiliating, and
eminently unjust to him, Tiburce. He would
have rejoiced if the most imperceptible gesture
had given him to understand that she was
touched by his love; he had already forgotten
that he was standing before a painting, so quick
is passion to attribute its own ardour even to
objects incapable of feeling it. Pygmalion
must have been astonished, as if it were a most
extraordinary thing, that this statue did not
return caress for caress; Tiburce was no less
shocked by the coldness of his painted sweetheart.

Kneeling in her robe of green satin, with its
ample and swelling folds, she continued to
gaze upon the Christ with an expression of

grief-stricken concupiscence, like a mistress
who seeks to surfeit herself with the features
of an adored face which she is never to see
again; her hair fell over her shoulders, a luminous fringe; a sunbeam, straying in by
chance, heightened the warm whiteness of
her linen and of her arms of gilded marble;
in the wavering light her breast seemed to
swell and throb with an appearance of life;
the tears in her eyes melted, and flowed like
human tears.

Tiburce thought that she was about to rise
and step down from the picture.

Suddenly there was darkness: the vision
vanished.

The English visitors had withdrawn, after
observing: "Very well; a pretty picture";
and the beadle, annoyed by Tiburce's prolonged contemplation, had closed the shutters,
and was demanding the usual fee. Tiburce
gave him all that he had in his pocket; lovers
are generous to duennas; the Antwerpian
beadle was the Magdalen's duenna, and

Tiburce, already looking forward to another interview, was interested in obtaining his favourable consideration.

The colossal St. Christopher, and the hermit carrying a lantern, painted on the exterior of the shutters, albeit very remarkable works, were far from consoling Tiburce for the closing of that dazzling tabernacle, whence the genius of Rubens sparkles like a monstrance laden with precious stones.

He left the church, carrying in his heart the barbed arrow of an impossible love; he had at last fallen in with the passion that he sought, but he was punished where he had sinned: he had become too fond of painting, he was doomed to love a picture. Nature, neglected for art, revenged herself in barbarous fashion; the most timid lover, in the presence of the most virtuous of women, always retains a secret hope in a corner of his heart; as for Tiburce, he was sure of his mistress's resistance and he was perfectly well aware that he would never be happy;

so that his passion was a genuine passion, a wild, insensate passion, capable of anything; it was especially remarkable for its disinterestedness.

Do not make too merry over Tiburce's love; how many men do we see deeply enamoured of women whom they have never seen except in a box at the theatre, to whom they have never spoken, and even the sound of whose voice they do not know! Are such men much more reasonable than our hero, and are their impalpable idols to be compared with the Magdalen at Antwerp?

Tiburce walked the streets with a proud and mysterious air, like a gallant returning from a first assignation. The intensity of his sensations surprised him agreeably — he who had never lived except in the brain felt the beating of his heart. It was a novel sensation; and so he abandoned himself without reserve to the charms of that unfamiliar impression; a real woman would not have touched him so deeply. An artificial man can be moved only by an artificial thing; there is a harmony between them; the true would create a discord. As we have said, Tiburce had read much, seen much, thought much, and felt very little; his fancies were simply brain fancies; in him passion rarely went below the cravat. But this time he was really in love, just like a student of rhetoric; the dazzling image of the Magdalen floated before his eyes in luminous spots, as if he had been looking at the sun; the slightest fold, the most imperceptible detail stood out clearly in his memory; the picture was always present before him. He tried in all seriousness to devise some means to impart life to that insensible beauty and to induce her to come forth from her frame; he thought of Prometheus, who kindled the fire of heaven in order to give a soul to his lifeless work; of Pygmalion, who succeeded in finding a way to move and warm a block of marble; he had an idea of plunging into the bottomless ocean of the occult sciences, in order to discover a charm sufficiently powerful to give life and substance to that vain appearance. He raved, he was mad: he was in love, you see.

Have not you yourself, without reaching that pitch of excitement, been invaded by a feeling of indescribable melancholy in a gallery of old masters, while thinking of the vanished beauties represented by their pictures? Would not one be glad to infuse life into all those pale and silent faces which seem to muse sadly against the greenish ultramarine or the coal-black which forms the background? Those eyes, whose vital spark gleams more brightly beneath the veil of age, were copied from those of a young princess or a lovely courtesan, of whom naught remains, not even a single grain of dust; those lips, half parted in a painted smile, recall real smiles forever fled. What a pity, in truth, that the women of Raphael, of Correggio, and of Titian are but impalpable shades! And why have not the models, like their portraits, received the

privilege of immortality? The harem of
the most voluptuous sultan would be a small
matter compared with that which one might
form with the odalisques of painting, and it
is really to be regretted that so much beauty
is lost.

Tiburce went every day to the cathedral,
and lost himself in contemplation of his beloved Magdalen; and he returned to the hotel
each evening, more in love, more depressed,
and more insane than ever. More than one
noble heart, even without caring for pictures,
has known the sufferings of our friend, when
trying to breathe his soul into some lifeless
idol, who had only the outward phantom of
life, and realised the passion she inspired no
more than a coloured figure.

With the aid of powerful glasses our lover
scrutinised his inamorata even in the most
imperceptible details. He admired the fineness of the flesh, the solidity and suppleness
of the colouring, the energy of the brush, the
vigour of the drawing, as another would ad-

mire the velvety softness of the skin, the whiteness and the beautiful colouring of a living mistress. On the pretext of examining the work at closer range, he obtained a ladder from his friend, the beadle, and, all aquiver with love, he dared to rest a presumptuous hand on the Magdalen's shoulder. He was greatly surprised to feel, instead of the satin-like softness of a woman's flesh, a hard, rough surface like a file, with hollows and ridges everywhere, due to the impetuosity of the impulsive painter's brush. This discovery greatly depressed Tiburce, but, as soon as he had descended to the floor again, his illusion returned.

He passed more than a fortnight thus, in a state of transcendental enthusiasm, wildly stretching out his arms to his chimera, imploring Heaven to perform a miracle. In his lucid moments he resigned himself to the alternative of seeking throughout the city some type approaching his ideal; but his search resulted in nothing, for one does not find readily on streets and public promenades such a diamond of beauty.

One evening, however, he met again, at the corner of Meïr Square, the charming blue glance we have previously mentioned; this time the vision disappeared less quickly, and Tiburce had time to see a lovely face framed by rich clusters of fair hair, and an artless smile playing about the freshest lips in the world. She quickened her pace when she realised that she was followed, but Tiburce, keeping at a distance, saw her stop in front of a respectable old Flemish house, of poor but decent aspect. As there was some delay in admitting her, she turned for an instant, doubtless in obedience to a vague instinct of feminine coquetry, to see if the stranger had been discouraged by the long walk she had compelled him to take. Tiburce, as if enlightened by a sudden gleam of light, saw that she bore a striking resemblance to—the Magdalen.

The Fleece of Gold

III

THE house which the slender figure had
entered had an air of Flemish simplicity altogether patriarchal. It was painted a
faded rose-colour, with narrow white lines to
represent the joints of the stones. The gable,
denticulated like the steps of a staircase; the
roof with its round windows surrounded by
scrollwork; the impost, representing, with
true Gothic artlessness, the story of Noah de-
rided by his sons; the stork's nest, and the
pigeons making their toilet in the sun, made
it a perfect example of its type; you would
have said that it was one of those factories so
common in the pictures of Van der Heyden
and of Teniers.

A few stalks of hops softened with their
playful greenery the too severe and too
methodical aspect of the house as a whole.
The lower windows were provided with
rounded bars, and over the two lower panes
were squares of muslin embroidered with

great bunches of flowers after the Brussels fashion; in the space left empty by the swelling of the iron bars were china pots containing a few pale carnations of sickly aspect, despite the evident care the owner took of them; for their drooping heads were supported by playing-cards and a complicated system of tiny scaffoldings of twigs of osier. Tiburce observed this detail, which indicated a chaste and restrained life, a whole poem of youth and beauty.

As, after two hours of waiting, he had not seen the fair Magdalen with the blue eyes come forth, he sagely concluded that she must live there; which was true. All that he had left to do was to learn her name, her position in society, to become acquainted with her, and to win her love; mere trifles, in very truth. A professional Lovelace would not have been delayed five minutes; but honest Tiburce was not a Lovelace; on the contrary, he was bold in thought, but timid in action; no one was less clever than he at passing from the general to the particular, and in love affairs he had a most pressing need of a trustworthy Pandarus to extol his perfections and to arrange his rendezvous. Once under way, he did not lack eloquence; he declaimed the languorous harangue with due self-possession, and played the lover at least as well as a provincial *jeune premier;* but, unlike Petit-Jean, the dog's lawyer, the part that he was least expert at was the beginning.

We are bound to admit, therefore, that worthy Tiburce swam in a sea of uncertainty, devising a thousand stratagems more ingenious than those of Polybius, to gain access to his divinity. As he found nothing suitable, he conceived the idea, like Don Cléofas in the *Diable Boiteux,* of setting fire to the house, in order to have an opportunity to rescue his darling from the flames and thus to prove to her his courage and his devotion; but he reflected that a fireman, more accustomed than he to roam about on burning rafters, might supplant him; and, moreover, that that method of making a pretty girl's acquaintance was forbidden by the Code.

Awaiting a better inspiration, he engraved very clearly on his brain the location of the house, noted the name of the street, and returned to his hotel, reasonably content, for he had imagined that he saw vaguely outlined behind the embroidered muslin at the window the graceful silhouette of the unknown, and a tiny hand put aside a corner of the transparent fabric, doubtless to make sure of his virtuous persistence in standing sentry, without hope of being relieved, at the corner of a lonely street in Antwerp. Was this mere conceit on the part of Tiburce, and was his *bonne fortune* one of those common to near-sighted men, who mistake linen hanging in the window for the scarf of Juliet leaning over towards Romeo, and pots of flowers for princesses in gowns of gold brocade? However that may have been, he went away in high spirits, looking upon himself as one of the most triumphant of gallants. The host-

The Fleece of Gold

ess of the Arms of Brabant and her black
maidservant were surprised at the airs of
Hamilcar and of a drum-major which he assumed. He lighted his cigar in the most determined fashion, crossed his legs, and began
to dandle his slipper on his toes with the
superb nonchalance of a mortal who utterly
despises all creation, and who is blest with
joys unknown to the ordinary run of man-
kind; he had at last found the blonde. Jason
was no happier when he took the marvellous
fleece from the enchanted tree.

Our hero was in the best of all possible
situations: a genuine Havana cigar in his
mouth, slippers on his feet, a bottle of Rhine
wine on his table, with the newspapers of
the past week and a pretty little pirated edition
of the poems of Alfred de Musset.

He could drink a glass, or even two, of
Tokay, read *Namouna,* or an account of the
latest ballet; there is no reason, therefore, why
we should not leave him alone for a few
moments; we have given him enough to

dispel his ennui, assuming that a lover can
ever suffer from ennui. We will return without him — for he is not the sort of a man to
open the doors for us — to the little house on
Rue Kipdorp, and we will act as introducers,
we will show you what there is behind the
embroidered muslin of the lower windows;
for, as our first piece of information, we will
tell you that the heroine of this tale lived on
the ground floor and that her name was
Gretchen; a name which, albeit not so eu-
phonious as Ethelwina, or Azalia, seemed
sufficiently sweet to German or Dutch ears.

Enter, after carefully wiping your feet, for
Flemish cleanliness reigns despotically here.
In Flanders, people wash their faces only
once a week, but by way of compensation
the floors are scalded and scraped to the quick
twice a day. The floor in the hall, like those
in the rest of the house, is made of pine boards,
whose natural colour is retained, the long, pale
veins and the starlike knots being hidden
by no varnish; it is sprinkled with a light

coating of sea-sand, carefully sifted, the grains of which hold the feet and prevent the slipping so frequent in our salons, where one skates rather than walks. Gretchen's bedroom is at the right, behind that door painted a modest gray, whose copper knob, scoured with pumice, shines as if it were of gold; rub your feet once more upon this mat of rushes; the emperor himself might not enter with muddy feet.

Observe an instant this placid and peaceful interior; there is nothing to attract the eye; everything is calm, sober, restrained; the chamber of Marguerite herself produces no more virginal impression; it is the serenity of innocence which presides over all these petty details so fascinatingly neat.

The brown walls, with an oaken wainscoting waist-high, have no other ornament than a Madonna in coloured plaster, dressed in real fabrics like a doll, with satin shoes, a wreath of rushes, a necklace of coloured glass, and two small vases of artificial flowers in front of her. At the rear of the room, in the corner most in the shadow, stands a four-posted bed of antique shape, with curtains of green serge and valances with pinked edges and a hem of yellow lace. By the pillow, a figure of the Christ, the lower part of the cross forming a holy-water vessel, stretches His ivory arms above the chaste maiden's slumbers.

A chest which glistens like a mirror, so diligently is it rubbed; a table with twisted legs standing near the window, and covered with spools, skeins of silk, and all the paraphernalia of lacework; a huge, upholstered easy-chair, three or four high-backed chairs of the style of Louis XIII., such as we see in the engravings of Abraham Bosse, composed the furnishing, almost puritanical in its simplicity.

We must add, however, that Gretchen, innocent as she was, had indulged in the luxury of a Venetian mirror, with bevelled edges, surrounded by a frame of ebony encrusted with copper. To be sure, to sanctify

that profane object, a twig of blessed boxwood was stuck in the frame.

Imagine Gretchen sitting in the great upholstered easy-chair, with her feet upon a
stool embroidered by herself, entangling and
disentangling with her fairy fingers the almost
imperceptible network of a piece of lace just
begun; her pretty head leaning over her work
is lighted from below by a thousand frolic-
some reflections which brighten with fresh
and vapoury tints the transparent shadow in
which she is bathed; a delicate bloom of
youth softens the somewhat too Dutch ruddi-
ness of her cheeks, whose freshness the half-
light cannot impair; the daylight, admitted
sparingly through the upper panes, touches
only the top of her brow, and makes the
little wisps of hair that rebel against the restraint of the comb gleam like golden tend-
rils. Cause a sudden ray of sunlight to play
upon the cornice and upon the chest, sprinkle
dots of gold over the rounded sides of the
pewter pots, make the Christ a little yellower;

retouch with a deeper shadow the stiff, straight folds of the serge curtains; darken the modernised pallor of the window-glass; stand old Barbara, armed with her broom, at the end of the room; concentrate all the light upon the maiden's head and hands, and you will have a Flemish painting of the best period, which Terburg or Gaspard Netscher would not refuse to sign.

What a contrast between that interior, so clean and neat and so easily understood, and the bedroom of a young Frenchwoman, always filled with clothes, with music-paper, with unfinished water-colours; where every article is out of its place; where tumbled dresses hang on the backs of chairs; and where the household cat tears with her claws the novel carelessly left on the floor! How clear and crystalline is the water in which that half-withered rose stands! How white that linen, how clear and transparent that glassware! Not a particle of dust in the air, not a rug out of place.

The Fleece of Gold

Metzu, who painted in a summer-house situated in the centre of a lake, in order to preserve the integrity of his colours, might have worked without annoyance in Gretchen's bedroom. The iron back of the fireplace shines like a silver bas-relief.

At this point a sudden apprehension seizes us; is she really the heroine suited to our hero? Is Gretchen really Tiburce's ideal? Is not all this very minute, very commonplace, very practical? is it not rather the Dutch than the Flemish type, and do you really believe that Rubens's models were built like her? Was it not rather merry gossips, highly-coloured, abounding in flesh, of robust health, and careless and vulgar manners, whose commonplace reality the painter's genius has idealised? The great masters often play us such tricks. Of an indifferent site they make a lovely landscape; of an ugly maidservant, a Venus; they do not copy what they see, but what they desire.

And yet Gretchen, although daintier and

more refined, really bore a striking resemblance to the Magdalen of Antwerp Cathedral,
and Tiburce's imagination might well rest
upon her without going astray. It would
have been hard for him to find a more magnificent body for the phantom of his painted
mistress.

You desire doubtless, now that you know
Gretchen and her bedroom, the bird and its
nest, as well as we ourselves do, to have some
details concerning her life and her social position. Her history was as simple as possible:
Gretchen was the daughter of small trades-
people who had been unfortunate, and she
had been an orphan for several years; she
lived with Barbara, a devoted old servant,
upon a small income, the remains of her
father's property, and upon the proceeds of
her work; as Gretchen made her own dresses
and her laces, as she was looked upon by the
Flemings as a prodigy of prudence and neat-
ness, she was able, although a simple working-girl, to dress with a certain elegance, and

The Fleece of Gold

to differ little from the daughters of citizens
of the middle class; her linen was fine, her
caps were always notable for their whiteness;
her boots were the best made in the city; for
—we trust that this detail will not displease
Tiburce — we must admit that Gretchen had
the foot of a Spanish countess, and shod herself to correspond. She was a well-educated
girl; she knew how to read, could write well,
knew all possible stitches in embroidery, had
no rival on earth in needlework, and did not
play the piano. Let us add that she had by
way of compensation an admirable talent for
cooking pear-tarts, carp *au bleu,* and cake; for
she prided herself on her culinary skill, like all
good housekeepers, and knew how to prepare
a thousand little delicacies after her own
recipes.

These details will seem without doubt far
from aristocratic, but our heroine is neither a
princess of diplomacy, nor a charming woman
of thirty, nor a fashionable singer; she is a
simple working-girl of Rue Kipdorp, near the

ramparts, Antwerp; but as, in our eyes, women have no real distinction save their beauty,
Gretchen is the equal of a duchess who is
entitled to sit in the king's presence, and
we look upon her sixteen years as sixteen
quarterings of nobility.

What was the state of Gretchen's heart?
The state of her heart was most satisfactory;
she had never loved anything but coffee-coloured turtle-doves, goldfish, and other absolutely innocent small creatures, which could
not cause the most savagely jealous lover a
moment's anxiety. Every Sunday she went
to hear high mass at the Jesuits' church,
modestly wrapped in her hood and attended
by Barbara carrying her book; then she went
home and turned over the leaves of a Bible,
"in which God the Father was represented
in the costume of an emperor," and of which
the wood-engravings aroused her admiration
for the thousandth time. If the weather was
fine, she went out to walk to Lillo fort, or
to the Head of Flanders, with a girl of her

own age, also a laceworker. During the week she seldom went out, except to deliver her work; and Barbara undertook that duty most of the time. A girl of sixteen years who has never thought of love would be an improbable character in a warmer climate; but the atmosphere of Flanders, made heavy by the sickly exhalations from the canals, contains very few aphrodisiac molecules; the flowers are backward there, and when they come are thick and pulpy; their odours, laden with moisture, resemble the odours of decoctions of aromatic herbs; the fruits are watery; the earth and the sky, saturated with moisture, send back and forth the vapours which they cannot absorb, and which the sun tries in vain to drink with its pale lips; the women who live in this bath of mist have no difficulty in being virtuous, for, according to Byron, that rascal of a sun is a great seducer and has made more conquests than Don Juan.

It is not surprising, therefore, that Gretchen, in such a moral atmosphere, was a perfect

stranger to all ideas of love, even under the
form of marriage, a legal and permissible form
if such there be.   She had read no bad novels,
nor even any good ones; she had not any
male relatives, cousins or second cousins.
Lucky Tiburce!   Moreover, the sailors with
their short, coloured pipes, the captains of the
East-Indiamen, who strolled about the city
during their brief time on shore, and the dignified merchants who went to the Bourse,
revolving figures in the wrinkles of their fore-
heads, and who cast their fleeting shadows
into Gretchen's sanctum as they walked by
the house, were not at all calculated to inflame
the imagination.

Let us admit, however, that, despite her
maidenly ignorance, the lace-worker had
remarked Tiburce as a well-turned cavalier
with regular features; she had seen him
several times at the cathedral, in rapt contemplation before the *Descent from the Cross,*
and attributed his ecstatic attitude to an excessive piety most edifying in so young a

man. As she whirled her bobbins about, she thought of the stranger of Meïr Square, and abandoned herself to innocent reverie. One day even, under the influence of that thought, she rose, and unconscious of her own act, went to her mirror, which she consulted for a long while; she looked at herself full-faced, in profile, in all possible lights, and discovered — what was quite true — that her complexion was more silky than a sheet of rice or camellia paper; that she had blue eyes of a marvellous limpidity, charming teeth in a mouth as red as a peach, and fair hair of the loveliest shade. She noticed for the first time her youthful charm and her beauty; she took the white rose which stood in the pretty glass, placed it in her hair, and smiled to see how that simple flower embellished her; coquetry was born and love would soon follow it.

But it is a long time since we left Tiburce; what had he been doing at the Arms of Brabant, while we furnished this information concerning the lace-worker? He had written upon a very fine sheet of paper what was probably a declaration of love, unless it was a challenge; for several other sheets, besmeared and marred by erasures, which lay on the floor, proved that it was a document very difficult to draw up, and of great importance. After finishing it, he took his cloak and bent his steps once more towards Rue Kipdorp.

Gretchen's lamp, a star of peace and toil, shone softly behind the glass, and the shadow of the girl as she leaned over her work was cast upon the transparent muslin. Tiburce, more excited than a robber about to turn the key of a treasure-chest, drew near the window with the step of a wolf, passed his hand through the bars, and buried in the soft earth of the vase of carnations the corner of his letter thrice folded, hoping that Gretchen could not fail to see it when she opened her window in the morning to water her flowers. That done, he withdrew with a step as light as if the soles of his boots were covered with felt.

The Fleece of Gold

IV

THE fresh blue light of the morning paled the sickly yellow of the lanterns, which were almost burned out; the Scheldt steamed like a sweating horse, and the daylight was beginning to filter through the rents in the mist, when Gretchen's window opened. Gretchen's eyes were still swimming in languor, and the mark left on her delicate cheek by a fold of the pillow showed that she had slept without moving in her little virginal bed, that profound sleep of which youth alone has the secret. She was anxious to see how her dear carnations had passed the night, and had hastily wrapped herself in the first garment that came to hand; that graceful and modest *déshabillé* became her wondrously; and if the idea of a goddess can be reconciled with a little cap of Flanders linen embellished with lace, and a dressing-sack of white dimity, we will venture to say that she had the aspect of Aurora opening the gates of the East; this comparison is perhaps a little too majestic for a lace-worker who is about to water a garden contained in two porcelain pots; but surely Aurora was less fresh and rosy, especially the Aurora of Flanders, whose eyes are always a little dull.

Gretchen, armed with a large pitcher, prepared to water her carnations, and Tiburce's ardent declaration came very near being drowned beneath a moral deluge of cold water; luckily the white paper caught Gretchen's eye; she disinterred the letter and was greatly surprised when she saw its contents. There were only two sentences, one in French, the other in German; the French sentence was composed of two words, "je t'aime"; the German of three, "ich liebe dich"; which means exactly the same thing. Tiburce had provided for the possibility that Gretchen would understand only her mother tongue; he was, as you see, a consummately prudent person.

Really, it was well worth while to besmear

more paper than Malherbe ever used to compose a stanza, and to drink, on the pretext of exciting the imagination, a bottle of excellent Tokay, in order to arrive at that ingenious and novel thought. But, despite its apparent simplicity, Tiburce's letter was perhaps a masterpiece of libertinism, unless it was mere folly, which is possible. However, was it not a master-stroke to let fall thus, like a drop of melted lead, into the midst of that tranquillity of mind that single phrase, "I love you"? And was not its fall certain to produce, as on the surface of a lake, an infinite number of radiations and concentric circles?

In truth, what do all the most ardent love-letters contain? What remains of all the bombast of passion when one pricks it with the pin of reason? All the eloquence of Saint-Preux reduces itself to a phrase; and Tiburce had really attained great profundity by concentrating in that brief sentence the flowery rhetoric of his first draughts.

He did not sign it; indeed, what information would his name have given ? He was a stranger in the city, he did not know Gretchen's name, and, to tell the truth, cared very little about it. The affair was more romantic, more mysterious thus; the least fertile imagination might build thereupon twenty octavo volumes more or less probable. Was he a sylph, a pure spirit, a love-lorn angel, a handsome officer, a banker's son, a young nobleman, a peer of England with an income of a million, a Russian feudal lord, with a name ending in *off,* many roubles, and a multitude of fur collars ? Such were the serious questions which that laconically eloquent letter must inevitably raise. The familiar form of address, which is used only to Divinity, betrayed a violence of passion which Tiburce was very far from feeling, but which might produce the best effect upon the girl's mind, as exaggeration always seems more natural to a woman than the truth.

Gretchen did not hesitate an instant to

believe the young man of Meïr Square to be the author of the note; women never err in such matters; they have a wonderful instinct, a scent, which takes the place of familiarity with the world and knowledge of the passions. The most virtuous of them knows more than Don Juan with his list.

We have described our heroine as a very artless, very ignorant, and very respectable young woman; we must confess, however, that she did not feel the virtuous indignation which a woman ought to feel who receives a note written in two languages and containing such a decided incongruity. She felt rather a thrill of pleasure, and a faint pink flush passed over her face. That letter was to her like a certificate of beauty; it reassured her concerning herself, and gave her a definite rank; it was the first glance that had ever penetrated her modest obscurity; the small proportions of her fortune prevented her being sought in marriage. Thus far she had been considered simply as a child, Tiburce consecrated her a young woman; she felt for him such gratitude as the pearl must feel for the diver who discovers it in its coarse shell beneath the dark cloak of the ocean.

This first impression passed, Gretchen experienced a sensation well-known to all those who have been brought up strictly, and who never have had a secret; the letter embarrassed her like a block of marble; she did not know what to do with it. Her room seemed to her not to have enough dark corners, enough impenetrable hiding-places, in which to conceal it from all eyes. She put it in the chest behind a pile of linen; but after a few moments she took it out again; the letter blazed through the boards of the wardrobe like Doctor Faust's microcosm in Rembrandt's etching. Gretchen looked for another, safer place; Barbara might need napkins or sheets and might find it. She took a chair, stood upon it, and placed the letter on the canopy of her bed; the paper burned her hands like a piece of red-hot iron.

The Fleece of Gold

Barbara entered to arrange the room. Gretchen, affecting the most indifferent air imaginable, took her usual seat and resumed her work of the day before; but at every step that Barbara took towards the bed, she fell into a horrible fright; the arteries in her temples throbbed, the hot sweat of anguish stood upon her forehead, her fingers became entangled in the threads, and it seemed to her that an invisible hand was grasping her heart. Barbara seemed to her to have an uneasy, suspicious expression which was not customary with her. At last the old woman went out, with a basket on her arm, to do her marketing. Poor Gretchen breathed freely again, and took down her letter, which she put in her pocket; but soon it made her itch; the creaking of the paper terrified her, and she put it in her breast; for that is where a woman puts everything that embarrasses her. The waist of a dress is a cupboard without a key, an arsenal filled with flowers, locks of hair, lockets, and sentimental epistles; a sort

5 [65]

of letter-box, in which one mails all the correspondence of the heart.

But why did Gretchen not burn that insignificant scrap of paper which caused her such keen terror ? In the first place, Gretchen had never in her life experienced such poignant emotion; she was terrified and enchanted at once. And then, pray tell us why lovers persist in not destroying letters which may lead later to their detection and perdition ? It is because a letter is a visible soul; because passion has passed through that paltry sheet with its electric fluid, and has imparted life to it. To burn a letter is to commit a moral murder; in the ashes of a destroyed correspondence there are always some particles of two hearts.

So Gretchen kept her letter in the folds of her dress, beside a little gold crucifix, which was greatly surprised to find itself in close proximity to a love-letter.

Like a shrewd young man, Tiburce left his declaration time to work. He played the dead man and did not again appear in Rue Kipdorp. Gretchen was beginning to be alarmed, when one fine morning she perceived in the bars of her window a superb bouquet of exotic flowers. Tiburce had passed that way; that was his visiting-card.

The bouquet afforded much pleasure to the young working-girl, who had become accustomed to the thought of Tiburce, and whose self-esteem was secretly hurt by the small amount of zeal which he had shown after such an ardent beginning; she took the bunch of flowers, filled with water one of her pretty Saxon vases with a raised blue design, untied the stalks and put them in water, in order to keep them longer. On this occasion she told the first lie of her life, informing Barbara that the bouquet was a present from a lady to whom she had carried some lace, and who knew her liking for flowers.

During the day Tiburce came to cool his heels in front of the house, on the pretext of making a drawing of some odd bit of architecture; he remained for a long while, working with a blunt pencil on a piece of wretched vellum. Gretchen played the dead in her turn; not a fold stirred, not a window opened; the house seemed asleep. Entrenched in a corner, she was able by means of the mirror in her work-box to watch Tiburce at her ease. She saw that he was tall, well-built, with an air of distinction in his whole person, regular features, a soft and melting eye, and a melancholy expression, which touched her deeply, accustomed as she was to the rubicund health of Brabantine faces. Moreover, Tiburce, although he was neither a lion nor a dandy, did not lack natural refinement, and must have appeared an ultrafashionable to a young girl so innocent as Gretchen; on Boulevard de Gand he would have seemed hardly up-to-date, on Rue Kipdorp he was magnificent.

In the middle of the night, Gretchen, obeying an adorable childish impulse, rose and

went barefooted to look at her bouquet; she
buried her face in the flowers, and kissed
Tiburce on the red lips of a magnificent
dahlia; she thrust her head passionately into
the multicoloured waves of that bath of
flowers, inhaling with long breaths intox-
icating perfume, breathing with full nostrils,
until she felt her heart melt and her eyes
grow moist. When she stood erect, her
cheeks glistened with pearly drops, and her
fascinating little nose, smeared as prettily as
possible with the golden dust from the sta-
mens, was a lovely shade of yellow. She
wiped it laughingly, returned to bed and to
sleep; as you may imagine, she saw Tiburce
in all her dreams.

In all this what had become of the Magdalen of the *Descent from the Cross?* She
still reigned without a rival in our young
enthusiast's heart; she had the advantage
over the loveliest living woman of being
impossible; with her there was no disillusionment, no satiety; she did not break the

spell by commonplace or absurd phrases; she was always there, motionless, adhering religiously to the sovereign lines within which the great master had confined her; sure of being beautiful to all eternity; and relating to the world in her silent language the dream of a sublime genius.

The little lace-worker of Rue Kipdorp was truly a charming creature; but how far were her arms from having that undulating and supple contour, that potent energy, all enveloped with grace; how juvenile was the slender curve of her shoulders! and how pale the shade of her hair beside those strange, rich tones with which Rubens had warmed the rippling locks of the placid sinner! Such was the language which Tiburce used to himself as he walked upon the Quay of the Scheldt.

However, seeing that he made little progress in his love affair with the painting, he reasoned with himself most sensibly concerning his monumental folly. He returned to

Gretchen, not without a long-drawn sigh of regret; he did not love her, but at all events she reminded him of his dream, as a daughter reminds one of an adored mother who is dead. We will not dwell on the details of this little intrigue, for every one can easily imagine them. Chance, that great procurer, afforded our two lovers a very natural opportunity to speak.

Gretchen had gone as usual to the Head of Flanders on the other side of the Scheldt with her young friend. They had run after butterflies, made wreaths of blue-bottles, and rolled about on the straw in the mills, so long that night had come and the ferryman had made his last trip, unperceived by them. They were standing there, both decidedly perturbed, with one foot in the water, shouting with all the strength of their little silvery voices for him to come back and get them ; but the playful breeze carried their shouts away, and there was no reply save the soft splashing of the waves on the sand.

Luckily, Tiburce was drifting about in a small sailboat; he heard them and offered to take them across; an offer which the friend eagerly accepted, despite Gretchen's embarrassed air and her flushed cheeks. Tiburce escorted her home and took care to organise a boating party for the following Sunday, with the assent of Barbara, whom his assiduous attendance at the churches and his devotion to the picture of the *Descent from the Cross* had very favourably disposed.

Tiburce met with no great resistance on Gretchen's part. She was so pure that she did not defend herself, because she did not know that she was attacked; and besides, she loved Tiburce; for although he talked very jocosely and expressed himself upon all subjects with ironical heedlessness, she divined that he was unhappy, and a woman's instinct is to console: grief attracts them as a mirror attracts the lark.

Although the young Frenchman was most attentive to her and treated her with extreme

courtesy, she felt that she did not possess his
heart entirely, and that there were corners
in his mind to which she never penetrated.
Some hidden thought of superior moment
seemed to engross him and it was evident
that he made frequent journeys into an unknown world; his fancy, borne away by the
involuntary flappings of its wings, lost its
footing constantly and beat against the ceiling, seeking, like a captive bird, some issue
through which to dart forth into the blue
sky. Often he scrutinised her with extraordinary earnestness for hours at a time,
sometimes with a satisfied expression, and
again with an air of dissatisfaction. That
look was not the look of a lover. Gretchen
could not understand such behaviour, but as
she was sure of Tiburce's loyalty, she was
not alarmed.

Tiburce, on the pretext that Gretchen's
name was hard to pronounce, had christened
her Magdalen, a substitution which she had
gladly accepted, feeling a secret pleasure in

having her lover call her by a different and mysterious name, as if she were to him another woman. He still made frequent visits to the cathedral, teasing his mania by impotent contemplations; and on those days Gretchen paid the penalty for the harsh treatment of the Magdalen; the real had to pay for the ideal. He was cross, bored, tiresome, which the honest creature ascribed to irritated nerves or too persistent reading.

Nevertheless, Gretchen was a charming girl, who deserved to be loved on her own account. Not in all the divisions of Flanders, in Brabant or Hainault, could you find a whiter and fresher skin and hair of a lovelier shade; her hand was at once plump and slender, with nails like agate,— a genuine princess's hand; and—a rare perfection in the country of Rubens—a small foot.

Ah! Tiburce, Tiburce, who longed to hold in your arms a real ideal, and to kiss your chimera on the mouth, beware! Chimeras, despite their rounded throats, their swan's wings, and their sparkling smiles, have sharp teeth and tearing claws. The evil creatures will pump the pure blood from your heart, and leave you dryer and more hollow than a sponge; avoid that unbridled ambition, do not try to make marble statues descend from their pedestals, and do not address your supplications to dumb canvases; all your painters and your poets were afflicted with the same disease that you have; they tried to make creations of their own in the midst of God's creation. With marble, with colours, with the rhythm of verses, they translated and defined their dream of beauty; their works are not the portraits of their mistresses, but of the mistresses they longed for, and you would seek in vain their models on earth. Go and buy another bouquet for Gretchen, who is a sweet and lovely maiden; drop your dead women and your phantoms, and try to live with the people of this world.

V

YES, Tiburce, though it will surprise you greatly to learn it, Gretchen is vastly superior to you. She has never read the poets, and does not even know the names of Homer and Virgil; the lamentations of the Wandering Jew, of Henriette and Damon, printed on wood and roughly-coloured, compose all of her literature, except the Latin in her mass-book, which she spells out conscientiously every Sunday; Virginie knew little more in the solitude of her paradise of magnolias and roses.

You are, it is true, thoroughly posted in literary affairs. You are profoundly versed in æsthetics, esoterics, plastics, architectonics, and poetics; Marphurius and Pancratius had not a finer list of acquirements in *ics*. From Orpheus and Lycophron down to M. de Lamartine's last volume, you have devoured everything that is composed of metres, of rimed lines, and of strophes cast

in every possible mould; no romance has escaped you. You have traversed from end to
end the vast world of the imagination; you
know all the painters from Andrea Rico of
Crete, and Bizzamano, down to Messieurs
Ingres and Delacroix; you have studied
beauty at its purest sources; the bas-reliefs
of Ægina, the friezes of the Parthenon, the
Etruscan vases, the hieratic sculptures of
Egypt, Greek art and Roman art, the Gothic
and the Renaissance; you have searched and
analysed everything; you have become a sort
of jockey of Beauty, whose advice painters
take when they desire to select a model, as
one consults a groom concerning the pur-
chase of a horse. Certainly no one is more
familiar than you with the physical side of
woman; you are as expert as an Athenian
sculptor on that point; but poetry has engrossed you so much that you have sup-
pressed nature, the world, and life. Your
mistresses have been to you simply pictures
more or less satisfying; your love for the

beautiful and attractive ones was in the pro-
portion of a Titian to a Coucher or a Vanloo;
but you have never wondered whether anything real throbbed and vibrated beneath that
exterior. Although you have a kind heart,
grief and joy seem to you like two grimaces
which disturb the tranquillity of the outlines;
woman is in your eyes a warm statue.

Ah! unhappy child, throw your books
into the fire, tear your engraving, shatter
your plaster casts, forget Raphael, forget
Homer, forget Phidias, since you have not
the courage to take a pencil, a pen, or a
modelling-tool; of what use is this sterile
admiration to you? what will be the end
of these insane impulses? Do not demand
more of life than it can give you. Great
geniuses alone are entitled not to be content
with creation. They can go and look the
Sphinx squarely in the face, for they solve its
riddles. But you are not a great genius; be
simple of heart, love those who love you,
and, as Jean Paul says, do not ask for moon-

light, or for a gondola on Lake Maggiore, or
for a rendezvous at Isola Bella.

Become a philanthropic advocate or a con-
cierge, limit your ambition to becoming a
voter and a corporal in your company; have
what in the world is called a trade; become
an honest citizen. At these words no doubt
your long hair will stand erect in horror, for
you have the same scorn for the simple bourgeois that the German student professes for
the philistine, the soldier for the civilian, and
the Brahma for the Pariah. You crush with
ineffable disdain every worthy tradesman
who prefers a vaudeville song to a tercet of
Dante, and the muslin of fashionable portrait-
painters to a sketch by Michelangelo. Such
a man is in your eyes below the brute, and
yet there are plain citizens whose minds—
and they have minds—are rich with poetic
feeling, who are capable of love and devotion,
and who experience emotions of which you
are incapable, you whose brain has annihilated the heart.

Théophile Gautier

Look at Gretchen, who has done nothing but water carnations and make lace all her life; she is a thousand times more poetic than you, *monsieur l'artiste,* as they say nowadays; she believes, she hopes, she smiles, and weeps; a word from you brings sunshine or rain to her lovely face; she sits there in her great upholstered armchair, beside her window, in a melancholy light, at work upon her usual task; but how her young brain labours! how fast her imagination travels! how many castles in Spain she builds and throws down! See her blush and turn pale, turn hot and cold, like the amorous maiden of the ancient ode; her lace drops from her hands, she has heard on the brick sidewalk a step which she distinguishes among a thousand, with all the acuteness which passion gives to the senses; although you arrive at the appointed time, she has been waiting for you a long while. All day you have been her sole preoccupation; she has asked herself: "Where is he now?— What is he doing?—Is he thinking of me as I

am thinking of him?—Perhaps he is ill; yesterday he seemed to me paler than usual, and
he had a distressed and preoccupied expression when he left me; can anything have
happened to him? Has he received unpleasant news from Paris?"—and all those questions which love propounds to itself in its
sublime disquietude.

That poor child, with her great loving heart,
has displaced the centre of her existence, she
no longer lives except in you and through
you. By virtue of the wonderful mystery of
the incarnation of love, her soul inhabits your
body, her spirit descends upon you and visits
you; she would throw herself in front of the
sword which should threaten your breast; the
blow that should reach you would cause her
death; and yet you have taken her up simply
as a plaything, to use her as a manikin for
your ideal. To merit such a wealth of love,
you have darted a few glances at her, given
her a few bouquets, and declaimed in a passionate tone the commonplaces of romance.

A more earnest lover would have failed perhaps; for, alas! to inspire love, it is not
necessary to feel it one's self. You have de-
liberately disturbed for all time the limpidity
of that modest existence. Upon my word,
Master Tiburce, adorer of the blonde type and
contemner of the bourgeois, you have done a
cruel thing; we regret to be obliged to tell
you so.

Gretchen was not happy; she divined an
invisible rival between herself and her lover
and jealousy seized her; she watched Tiburce's
movements, and saw that he went only to his
hotel, the Arms of Brabant, and to the cathedral on Meïr Square. She was reassured.

"What is the matter with you," she asked
him once, "that you are always looking at
the figure of the Magdalen supporting the
Saviour's body in the picture of the *Descent
from the Cross?*"

"Because she looks like you," Tiburce replied.

Gretchen blushed with pleasure and ran to

the mirror to verify the accuracy of the comparison; she saw that she had the unctuous and glowing eyes, the fair hair, the arched forehead, the general shape of the saint's face.

"So that is the reason that you call me Magdalen and not Gretchen, or Marguerite, which is my real name?"

"Precisely so," replied Tiburce, with an embarrassed air.

"I would never have believed that I was so lovely," said Gretchen; "and it makes me very happy, for you will love me better for it."

Serenity returned for some time to the maiden's heart, and we must confess that Tiburce made virtuous efforts to combat his insane passion. The fear of becoming a monomaniac came to his mind; and to cut short that obsession he determined to return to Paris.

Before starting, he went to pay one last visit to the cathedral, and his friend the beadle opened the shutters of the *Descent from the Cross* for him.

The Magdalen seemed to him more sad and disconsolate than usual; great tears rolled down her pallid cheeks, her mouth was contracted by a spasm of grief, a bluish circle surrounded her melting eyes, the sunbeam had left her hair, and there was, in her whole attitude, an expression of despair and prostration; one would have said that she no longer believed in the resurrection of her beloved Lord. In truth, the Christ was that day of such a sallow, greenish hue that it was difficult to imagine that life could ever return to his decomposing flesh. All the other people in the picture seemed to share that feeling; their eyes were dull, their expressions mournful, and their halos gave forth only a leaden gleam; the livid hue of death had invaded that canvas formerly so warm and full of life.

Tiburce was deeply touched by the expression of supreme melancholy upon the Magdalen's face, and his resolution to depart was

shaken. He preferred to attribute it to a
secret sympathy rather than to a caprice of
the light. The weather was dull, the rain
cut the sky with slender threads, and a ray of
daylight, drenched with water and mist, forced
its way with difficulty through the glass,
streaming and beaten by the wing of the
squall; that reason was much too plausible to
be admitted by Tiburce.

"Ah!" he said to himself in an undertone,
quoting a verse of one of our young poets,
" 'How I would love thee to-morrow if thou
wert living!'—Why art thou only an impalpable ghost, attached forever to the meshes
of this canvas and held captive by this thin
layer of varnish? Why art thou the phantom
of life, without the power to live? What
does it profit thee to be lovely, noble, and
great, to have in thine eyes the flame of
earthly love and of divine love, and about thy
head the resplendent halo of repentance, being
simply a little oil and paint spread on canvas
in a certain way? Oh! lovely adored one,

turn towards me for an instant that glance, at once so soft and so dazzling; sinner, take pity upon an insane passion, thou, to whom love opened the gates of Heaven; descend from that frame, stand erect in thy long, green satin skirt; for it is a long while that thou hast knelt before the sublime scaffold; these holy women will guard the body without thee and will suffice for the death vigil. Come, Magdalen, come! thou hast not emptied all thy jars of perfume at the feet of the Divine Master; there must remain enough of nard and cinnamon in the bottom of thy onyx jar to renew the lustre of thy hair, dimmed by the ashes of repentance. Thou shalt have, as of yore, strings of pearls, negro pages, and coverlets of the purple of Sidon. Come, Magdalen, although thou hast been two thousand years dead, I have enough of youth and ardour to reanimate thy dust. Ah! spectre of beauty, let me but hold thee in my arms one instant, then let me die!"

A stifled sigh, as faint and soft as the wail

of a dove mortally wounded, echoed sadly in the air. Tiburce thought that the Magdalen had answered him.

It was Gretchen, who, hidden behind a pillar, had seen all, heard all, understood all. Something had broken in her heart; she was not loved.

That evening Tiburce came to see her; he was pale and depressed. Gretchen was as white as wax. The excitement of the morning had driven the colour from her cheeks, like the powder from the wings of a butterfly.

"I start for Paris to-morrow; will you come with me?"

"To Paris or elsewhere; wherever you please," replied Gretchen, in whom every shred of will-power seemed extinct; "shall I not be unhappy everywhere?"

Tiburce flashed a keen and searching glance at her.

"Come to-morrow morning; I will be ready; I have given you my heart and my life. Dispose of your servant."

She went with Tiburce to the Arms of Brabant, to assist him to make his preparations for departure; she packed his books, his linen, and his pictures, then she returned to her little room on Rue Kipdorp; she did not undress, but threw herself fully dressed upon her bed.

An unconquerable depression had seized upon her soul; everything about her seemed sad: the bouquets were withered in their blue glass vases, the lamp flickered and cast a dim and intermittent light; the ivory Christ bent His head in despair upon His breast, and the blessed boxwood assumed the aspect of a cypress dipped in lustral water.

The little Virgin from her little recess watched her in surprise with her enamel eyes; and the storm, pressing his knee against the window-pane, made the lead partitions groan and creak.

The heaviest furniture, the most unimportant utensils, wore an expression of intelligence and compassion; they cracked dolorously and gave forth mournful sounds. The easy-chair held out its long, unoccupied arms; the hop-vine on the trellis passed its little green hand familiarly through a broken pane; the kettle complained and wept among the ashes; the curtains of the bed fell in more lifeless and more distressed folds; the whole room seemed to understand that it was about to lose its young mistress. Gretchen called her old servant, who wept bitterly; she handed her her keys and the certificates of her little income, then opened the cage of her two coffee-coloured turtle-doves and set them free.

The next morning she was on her way to Paris with Tiburce.

VI

TIBURCE'S apartment greatly surprised the young Antwerp maiden, accustomed to Flemish strictness and method. That mixture of luxury and heedlessness upset all her ideas. For instance, a crimson velvet cover was thrown upon a wretched broken table; magnificent candelabra of the most ornate style, which would not have been out of place in the boudoir of a king's mistress, were supplied with paltry *bobèches* of common glass, which the candles, burning down to the very bottom, had burst; a china vase of beautiful material and workmanship and of great value had received a kick in the side, and its splintered fragments were held together by iron wire; exceedingly rare engravings before letter were fastened to the wall by pins; a Greek cap was on the head of an antique *Venus*, and a multitude of incongruous objects, such as Turkish pipes, narghiles, daggers, yataghans, Chinese shoes, and Indian slippers, encumbered the chairs and what-nots.

The painstaking Gretchen had no rest until all this was cleaned, neatly hung, and labelled; like God who made the world from chaos, she made of that medley a delightful apartment. Tiburce, who was accustomed to its confusion and who knew perfectly where things ought not to be, had difficulty at first in recognising his surroundings; but he ended by becoming used to it. The objects which he disarranged returned to their places as if by magic. He realised for the first time what comfort meant. Like all imaginative people, he neglected details. The door of his bed-room was gilded and covered with arabesques, but it had no weather-strips; like the genuine savage that he was, he loved splendour and not well-being; he would have worn, like the Orientals, waistcoats of gold brocade lined with towelling.

And yet, although he seemed to enjoy this more human and more reasonable mode of life, he was often sad and distraught; he would remain whole days upon his divan, flanked by two piles of cushions, with eyes closed and hands hanging, and not utter a word; Gretchen dared not question him, she was so afraid of his reply. The scene in the cathedral had remained engraved upon her memory, in painful and ineffacable strokes.

He continued to think of the Magdalen at

Antwerp; absence made her more beautiful in his sight; he saw her before him like a luminous apparition. An imaginary sunlight riddled her hair with rays of gold, her dress had the transparency of an emerald, her shoulders gleamed like Parian marble. Her tears had dried, and youth shone in all its bloom upon the down of her rosy cheeks; she seemed entirely consoled for the death of the Christ, whose bluish white foot she supported heedlessly, while she turned her face towards her earthly lover. The rigid outlines of sanctity were softened and had become undulating and supple; the sinner reappeared in the person of the penitent; her neckerchief floated more freely, her skirt swelled out in alluring and worldly folds, her arms were amorously outstretched, as if ready to seize a victim of love. The great saint had become a courtesan, and had transformed herself into a temptress. In a more credulous age Tiburce would have seen therein some underhand machination of him who

goes prowling about, "seeking whom he
may devour"; he would have believed that
the devil's claw was upon his shoulder and
that he was bewitched in due form.

How did it happen that Tiburce, beloved
by a charming young girl, simple of heart,
and endowed with intelligence, possessed of
beauty, youth, innocence, all the real gifts
which come from God, and which no one
can acquire, persisted in pursuing a mad
chimera, an impossible dream; and how could
that mind, so keen and powerful, have arrived
at such a degree of aberration? Such things
are seen every day; have we not, each one
of us in our respective spheres, been loved
obscurely by some humble heart, while we
sought more exalted loves? Have not we
trodden under foot a pale violet with its
timid perfume, while striding along with
lowered eyes towards a cold and gleaming star
which cast its ironic glance upon us from the
depths of infinity? Has not the abyss its
magnetism and the impossible its fascination?

One day Tiburce entered Gretchen's chamber carrying a bundle; he took from it a skirt and waist of green satin, made after the antique style, a chemisette of a shape long out of fashion, and a string of huge pearls. He requested Gretchen to put on those garments, which could not fail to be most becoming to her, and to keep them in the house; he told her by way of explanation that he was very fond of sixteenth-century costumes, and that by falling in with that fancy of his she would confer very great pleasure upon him. You will readily believe that a young girl did not need to be asked twice to try on a new gown; she was soon dressed, and when she entered the salon, Tiburce could not withhold a cry of surprise and admiration. He found something to criticise, however, in the head-dress, and, releasing the hair from the teeth of the comb, he spread it out in great curls over Gretchen's shoulders, like the Magdalen's hair in the *Descent from the Cross*. That done, he gave a different

[94]

twist to some folds of the skirt, loosened the laces of the waist, rumpled the neckerchief, which was too stiff and starchy, and, stepping back a few feet, contemplated his work.

Doubtless you have seen what are called living pictures, at some special performance. The most beautiful actresses are selected, and dressed and posed in such wise as to reproduce some familiar painting. Tiburce had achieved a masterpiece of that sort; you would have said that it was a bit cut from Rubens's canvas.

Gretchen made a movement.

"Don't stir, you will spoil the pose; you are so lovely thus!" cried Tiburce in a tone of entreaty.

The poor girl obeyed and remained motionless for several minutes. When she turned, Tiburce saw that her face was bathed in tears.

He realised that she knew all.

Gretchen's tears flowed silently down her cheeks, without contraction of the features, without effort, like pearls overflowing from

the too full cup of her eyes, lovely azure flowers of divine limpidity; grief could not mar
the harmony of her face, and her tears were
lovelier than another woman's smile.

Gretchen wiped them away with the back
of her hand, and leaning upon the arm of a
chair, she said in a voice tremulous and melting with emotion:

"Oh, how you have made me suffer,
Tiburce! Jealousy of a new sort wrung my
heart; although I had no rival, I was betrayed
none the less; you loved a painted woman,
she possessed your thoughts, your dreams,
she alone seemed fair to you, who saw only
her in all the world; plunged in that mad
contemplation, you did not even see that I
had wept. And I believed for an instant that
you loved me, whereas I was simply a dupli-
cate, a counterfeit of your passion! I know
well that in your eyes I am only an ignorant
little girl who speaks French with a German
accent that makes you laugh; my face pleases
you as a reminder of your imaginary mistress;

you see in me a pretty manikin which you drape according to your fancy; but I tell you the manikin suffers and loves you."

Tiburce tried to draw her to his heart, but she released herself and continued:

"You talked to me enchantingly of love, you taught me that I was lovely and charming to look upon, you pressed my hands and declared that no fairy had smaller ones, you said of my hair that it was more precious than a prince's golden cloak, and of my eyes that the angels came down from Heaven to look at themselves in them, and that they stayed so long that they were late in returning and were scolded by the good Lord; and all this in a sweet and penetrating voice, with an accent of truth that would have deceived those more experienced than I. Alas! my resemblance to the Magdalen in the picture kindled your imagination and gave you that artificial eloquence; she answered you through my mouth; I gave her the life that she lacks, and I served to complete your illusion. If I

have given you a few moments of happiness,
I forgive you for making me play this part.
After all, it is not your fault if you do not
know how to love, if the impossible alone
attracts you, if you long only for that which
you cannot attain. You are ambitious to
love, you are deceived concerning yourself,
you will never love. You must have perfection, the ideal and poesy — all those things
which do not exist. Instead of loving in a
woman the love that she has for you, of
being grateful to her for her devotion and for
the gift of her heart, you look to see if she resembles that plaster *Venus* in your study.
Woe to her if the outline of her brow has not
the desired curve! You are concerned about
the grain of her skin, the shade of her hair, the
fineness of her wrists and her ankles, but
never about her heart. You are not a lover,
poor Tiburce, you are simply a painter.
What you have taken for passion is simply
admiration for shape and beauty; you were
in love with the talent of Rubens, not with

the Magdalen; your vocation of painter stirred vaguely within you and produced those frantic outbursts which you could not control. Thence came all the degradation of your fantasy. I have discovered this, because I love you. Love is a woman's genius, her mind is not engrossed in selfish contemplation! Since I have been here I have turned over your books, I have read your poets, I have become almost a scholar. The veil has fallen from my eyes. I have discovered many things that I should never have suspected. Thus I have been able to read clearly in your heart. You used to draw, take up your pencils again. You must place your dreams upon canvas, and all this great agitation will calm down of itself. If I cannot be your mistress, I will at all events be your model."

She rang and told the servant to bring an easel, canvas, colours, and brushes.

When the servant had prepared everything, the chaste girl suddenly let her garments fall to the floor with sublime immodesty, and raising her hair, like Aphrodite coming forth from the sea, stood in the bright light.

"Am I not as lovely as your *Venus of Milo?*" she asked with a sweet little pout.

After two hours, the face was already alive and half protruding from the canvas; in a week it was finished. It was not a perfect picture, however; but an exquisite touch of refinement and of purity, a wonderful softness of tone, and the noble simplicity of the arrangement made it noteworthy, especially to connoisseurs. That slender white and fair-haired figure, standing forth in an unconstrained attitude against the twofold azure of the sky and the sea, and presenting herself to the world nude and smiling, had a reflection of antique poesy and recalled the best periods of Greek sculpture.

Tiburce had already forgotten the Magdalen of Antwerp.

"Well!" said Gretchen, "are you satisfied with your model?"

The Fleece of Gold

"When would you like to publish our banns?" was Tiburce's reply.

"I shall be the wife of a great painter," she said, throwing her arms about her lover's neck; "but do not forget, monsieur, that it was I who discovered your genius, that priceless jewel—I, little Gretchen of Rue Kipdorp!"

1839.

Arria Marcella

Arria Marcella

A SOUVENIR OF POMPEII

THREE young men, three friends who were travelling in Italy together, visited last year the Studj Museum [1] at Naples, where the various antique objects exhumed from the ruins of Pompeii and Herculaneum are collected.

They had scattered through the rooms and were looking at the mosaics, the bronzes, the frescoes taken from the walls of the dead city, as their fancy led them; and when one of them found something especially interesting, he would call his companions with shouts of joy, to the great scandal of the taciturn English and the staid bourgeois, intent upon turning the leaves of their guide-books.

But the youngest of the three, having

---

[1] Now the Museo Nazionale ; formerly the Museo Borbonico, or Museo gli Studj.—[Trans.]

paused in front of a glass case, seemed not to hear his comrades' exclamations, so absorbed was he in profound contemplation. The object that he was examining so closely was a piece of coagulated black ashes, bearing a hollow impression; one would have said that it was a fragment of the mould of a statue, broken in the casting; the trained eye of an artist would easily have recognised the curve of a beautiful breast and of flanks as faultless in outline as those of a Greek statue. Every one knows, and the commonest traveller's guide will tell you, that the lava, cooling about a woman's body, had perpetuated its charming contours. Thanks to the caprice of an eruption which destroyed four cities, that noble form, fallen into dust nearly two thousand years ago, has come down to us; the rounded outline of a breast has lived through ages, when so many vanished empires have left no trace at all! That imprint of beauty, made by chance upon the scoria of a volcano, has not been effaced.

Arria Marcella

Seeing that he persisted in his contemplation, Octavian's two friends walked towards him, and Max, touching him on the shoulder, made him start like a man surprised in a secret. Evidently Octavian had heard neither Max nor Fabio approaching.

"Come, Octavian," said Max, "don't stand like this, whole hours in front of every case, or we shall miss the train, and shall not see Pompeii to-day."

"What on earth is the fellow looking at?" added Fabio, who had drawn near. "Ah! the imprint found in the house of Arrius Diomedes"; and he cast a rapid and peculiar glance at Octavian.

Octavian blushed slightly, took Max's arm, and the visit came to an end without other incidents. On leaving the Studj, the three friends entered a *corricolo* and were driven to the railway station. The *corricolo,* with its great red wheels, its seat studded with copper nails, its thin but high-spirited horse, harnessed like a Spanish mule, and galloping over the broad flagstones of lava, is too familiar for any description of it to be needed here; moreover, we are not writing impressions of a trip to Naples, but the simple narrative of a strange and incredible, but strictly true, adventure.

The railway to Pompeii skirts the sea almost all the way, and the long curls of foam break upon a blackish sand resembling sifted charcoal. The shore is in fact formed of streams of lava and volcanic ashes, and produces, by reason of its dark hue, a striking contrast to the blue of the sky and the blue of the water; amid all that brilliancy, the land alone seems to retain a shadow.

The villages which one passes through or skirts — Portici, made famous by M. Auber's opera, Resina, Torre del Greco, Torre dell'-Annunziata, whose houses with arcades and terraced roofs one sees in passing — have, despite the glare of the sun and the southern whitewash, a gloomy and grimy aspect, like Manchester and Birmingham; the dust is black, and an impalpable soot clings to everything; you realise that the mighty forge of Vesuvius is panting and smoking a few steps away.

The three friends alighted at the Pompeii station, laughing among themselves at the mixture of antique and modern which those words, "Pompeii Station," naturally bring to the mind. A Græco-Roman city and a railway terminus!

They crossed the field planted with cotton-trees, about which white tufts were fluttering, which separates the railway from the site of the disinterred city; and they took a guide at the inn built outside the former ramparts, or to speak more accurately, a guide took them; a calamity which it is difficult to avoid in Italy.

It was one of those lovely days which are so common in Naples, when, by virtue of the brilliancy of the sunlight and the transparency of the air, objects assume hues which seem fabulous in the north, and seem rather to belong to the world of dreams than to the world of reality. Whoever has once seen that gold and azure light carries away to his misty home an incurable homesickness for it.

The resuscitated city, having shaken off a corner of its winding-sheet of ashes, stood forth with its innumerable details, beneath a blinding glare. In the background rose the cone of Vesuvius, furrowed with streaks of blue, pink, and violet lava, gilded by the sun. A light mist, almost imperceptible in the glare, formed a hood for the crest of the mountain; at first one might have taken it for one of those clouds which, even in the loveliest weather, blot out the brow of lofty peaks. On looking more closely, one saw slender threads of white vapour emerge from the top of the mountain, as through the holes of a colander, and unite in a light smoke. The volcano, in a pleasant humour that day, was placidly smoking its pipe, and save for the example of Pompeii buried at its feet, one would not have believed it to be of a more

[110]

savage disposition than Montmartre. On the other side fair hills, with outlines voluptuously undulating like the hips of a woman, barred the horizon; and farther away the sea, that in other days bore biremes and triremes under the ramparts of the city, extended its azure boundary.

The aspect of Pompeii is most surprising; that abrupt backward leap of nineteen centuries astonishes even the prosaic and the least intelligent natures; two steps take you from antique to modern life, from Christianity to paganism; and so, when the three friends saw those streets, where the forms of a vanished existence are preserved intact, they were conscious, although prepared in a measure by books and pictures, of an impression as strange as it was profound. Octavian especially seemed stupefied, and followed the guide mechanically with the step of a sleepwalker, paying no heed to the monotonous catalogue, learned by heart, which that worthy recited like a lesson.

Théophile Gautier

He gazed with a startled eye at the waggon-ruts in the cyclopean pavement of the streets, which seem to date from yesterday, the impression is so fresh; at the inscriptions traced in red letters, in a running hand, on the walls: advertisements of plays, of houses to let, votive formulas, signs, announcements of all sorts; as curious and interesting as a blank wall of Paris, discovered two thousand years hence, with its advertisements and its placards, would be to the unknown people of the future; the houses with sunken roofs, allowing the eye to grasp all the household secrets, all those domestic details which historians neglect and the secret of which civilisations bear away with them; those fountains, hardly dry; that forum, surprised by the catastrophe in the midst of repairs, its pillars and architraves, all hewn and carved, waiting in all their purity of curve and angle to be put in place; the temples consecrated to gods now mythological, but who then had no unbelievers; the shops where only the tradesman is wanting; the wine-shops where the circular stain left by the drinker's glass may yet be seen on the marble; the barracks, with pillars painted with ochre and red lead, upon which the soldiers have scratched caricatures of men in combat; and the theatres for the drama and for concerts, placed side by side, which might resume their performances, were it not that the troupes which acted there, now reduced to the state of clay, are engaged perhaps in closing the bung-hole of a beer-cask, or stopping a crevice in a wall, like the dust of Alexander and Cæsar, according to the melancholy reflection of Hamlet.

Fabio mounted the stage of the tragic theatre, while Octavian and Max climbed to the highest bench; and there he began to declaim with abundant gestures such bits of poetry as came into his head, to the great alarm of the lizards, which scattered hither and thither, with quivering tails, and hid in the crevices of the ruined walls; and although the vessels of brass or earth, whose purpose was to repeat the sounds, no longer existed, his voice rang out none the less full and vibrant.

Then the guide led them across the tilled lands which cover those portions of Pompeii which are still buried, to the amphitheatre at the other end of the city. They walked beneath the trees whose roots forced their way through the roofs of buried buildings, loosened the tiles, split the ceilings, dislodged the pillars; and they passed through those fields where commonplace vegetables sprout above marvels of art, material tokens of the oblivion which time spreads over the loveliest things.

The amphitheatre did not surprise them. They had seen the one at Verona, which is larger and as well preserved, and they were as familiar with the arrangement of ancient arenas as with that of the scenes of bull-fights in Spain, which resemble them much, save in solidity of construction and beauty of materials.

Arria Marcella

So they retraced their steps, and taking a cross-street reached the Street of Fortune, listening with inattentive ear to the guide, who, as he passed each house, pointed it out by the name it was given at the time of its discovery, after some characteristic peculiarity: The House of the Bronze Bull, the House of the Faun, the House of the Ship, the Temple of Fortune, the House of Meleager, the Tavern of Fortune at the corner of the Consular Street, the Academy of Music, the Public Market, the Pharmacy, the Surgeon's Shop, the Custom-House, the Abode of the Vestals, the Inn of Albinus, the Thermopolium, and so on, to the gate leading to the Road of the Tombs.

That brick gate, covered with statues, and entirely denuded of ornamentation, has in its inner arch two deep grooves intended for the raising and lowering of a portcullis, like a donjon of the Middle Ages, to which one might well have supposed that that method of defence was peculiar.

"Who would have expected," said Max to his friends, "to find Pompeii, the Græco-Latin city, protected by a device so romantically Gothic? Can you imagine a belated Roman knight blowing his horn outside this gate, as a signal for the portcullis to be lifted, like a page of the fifteenth century?"

"There is nothing new under the sun," replied Fabio; "and even that aphorism itself is not new, as it was formulated by Solomon."

"Perhaps there is something new under the moon!" suggested Octavian, smiling with melancholy irony.

"My dear Octavian," said Max, who during this brief conversation had stopped before an inscription written in red chalk on the outer wall, "would you like to see a gladiatorial combat? Here are the notices: 'Combat and hunt on the fifth day of the nones of April; poles will be erected; twenty pairs of gladiators will fight on the nones'; and if you have any fear for the whiteness of your complexion, set your mind at rest, for sails will be stretched; unless you prefer to go to the amphitheatre early, for these fellows are to cut one another's throats in the morning — *matutini erunt;* nothing could be more considerate."

Chatting thus, the three friends followed that sepulchre-fringed road which, according to our modern ideas, would be a lugubrious promenade for a city, but which did not present the same melancholy meaning to the ancients, whose tombs contained, instead of ghastly dead bodies, only a pinch of ashes, an abstract idea of death. Art beautified these last resting-places, and, as Goethe says, the pagan decorated sarcophagi and urns with images of life.

That doubtless was the reason that Max and Fabio inspected with light-hearted curiosity and a joyous plenitude of life, which they would not have had in a Christian cemetery, those funeral monuments so gaily gilded by the sun, which, placed along the roadside,

seemed still to be related to life, and inspired none of that chill repulsion, none of
that fantastic terror which our gloomy places
of burial arouse. They paused before the
tomb of Mammia, the public priestess, near
which a tree has sprung up, a cypress or a
willow; they seated themselves in the semi-
circle of the triclinium, set apart for funeral
banquets, laughing like heirs; they read, with
many a jest, the epitaphs of Nevoleia, of
Labeon, and of the Arria family; followed by
Octavian, who seemed more touched than his
heedless companions by the fate of those dead
of two thousand years ago.

Thus they reached the villa of Arrius Diomedes, one of the most extensive dwelling-
houses in Pompeii. They went up to it by
brick steps, and when they had passed through
the gate flanked by two small pillars at the
sides, they found themselves in a courtyard,
like the patio which forms the centre of
Spanish and Moorish houses, and which the
ancients called the *impluvium,* or the *cavæ-*

dium; fourteen pillars, of brick covered with stucco, formed a portico or covered peristyle on all four sides, like the cloister of a convent; beneath it one could walk without fear of the rain. The pavement of the courtyard was a mosaic of brick and white marble, the effect of which was soft and pleasant to the eye. In the centre a four-sided marble basin, which still exists, received the rain-water which dripped from the portico. It produces a strange effect to enter thus the life of olden times, and to tread with patent leathers marble pavements worn by the sandals and buskins of the contemporaries of Augustus and Tiberius.

The guide led them through the *exedra,* or summer parlour, open towards the sea to admit the cool breezes. It was there that they received guests, and took their siesta during those burning hours when the south wind blew from Africa, laden with languor and tempest. He took them into the basilica, a long open gallery which furnished light to the apartments, and where visitors and clients

waited for the *nomenclator* to summon them;
then he led them out on the white marble
terrace, whence there was a prospect of green
gardens and blue sea; then he showed them
the *nymphæum,* or baths, with its walls
painted yellow, its stucco pillars, its mosaic
pavement, and its marble tub, which received
so many lovely bodies now vanished like
ghosts; the *cubiculum,* the scene of so many
dreams that flitted from the Ivory Gate, with
its alcoves hollowed out of the wall and
closed by a *conopeum,* or curtain, whose
bronze rings still lay on the ground; the
recreation-room; the chapel of the household
gods; the cabinet of archives; the library;
the gallery of pictures; the *gyneceum,* or women's apartment, consisting of small, partly
ruined rooms, the walls of which retain traces
of paintings and arabesques, like cheeks from
which the rouge has been imperfectly removed.

This inspection concluded, they went down
to the lower floor, for the ground is much

lower towards the garden than towards the Street of the Tombs; they passed through eight rooms painted in antique red, one of which had recesses in the walls, such as we see in the vestibule of the Hall of the Ambassadors at the Alhambra; and they arrived at last at a sort of cellar, the use of which was clearly indicated by the sight of eight earthen amphoræ propped against the wall, which doubtless were once perfumed, like the *Odes* of Horace, with Cretan wine, Falernian, and Massican.

A bright sunbeam entered through a small air-hole, half choked by nettles, whose leaves, pierced with light, it changed into emeralds and topazes; and that cheerful touch of nature smiled opportunely amid the depressing gloom of the place.

" This," said the guide in his droning voice, the tone of which accorded ill with his words, " this is where they found, among seventeen skeletons, that of the lady whose mould is shown in the museum at Naples. She had gold rings on her fingers, and pieces of her fine tunic were found stuck to the mass of ashes which retained her shape."

The guide's commonplace phrases deeply affected Octavian. He asked to see the exact spot where those precious remains had been discovered; and if he had not been restrained by the presence of his friends, he would have abandoned himself to some extravagant outburst; his bosom swelled, his eyes glistened with furtive moisture; that catastrophe, effaced by twenty centuries of oblivion, affected him like a disaster of recent occurrence; the death of a mistress or of a friend would not have distressed him more, and a tear two thousand years late fell, while Max and Fabio had their backs turned, upon the spot where that woman, of whom he felt enamoured with a retrospective love, breathed her last, suffocated by the hot cinders from the volcano.

"Enough of this archæology!" cried Fabio; "we don't expect to write a dissertation on a jug or a tile of the time of Julius Cæsar, in order to become a member of some provincial academy; these classic souvenirs make my stomach hollow. Let us go to dinner, that is, if it is possible, at that picturesque inn, where I am afraid they will serve us with fossil beefsteaks, and fresh eggs laid prior to the death of Pliny."

"I will not exclaim with Boileau:

"A fool sometimes delivers wise opinions,"

said Max, laughing, "for that would be impolite; but your idea is a good one. It would have been pleasanter, however, to banquet here, in somebody's triclinium, reclining in the ancient style, and served by slaves like Lucullus or Trimalchio. To be sure, I do not see many oysters from Lake Lucrinus; the turbot and mullet from the Adriatic are wanting; there is no Apulian boar in the market; and the loaves and the honey-cakes are in the museum at Naples, as hard as stones, beside their corroded moulds; raw macaroni, covered with *caccia-cavallo,* detestable as it may be, is better than nothing. What does dear Octavian think about it ?"

Octavian, who deeply regretted that he was not at Pompeii on the day of the eruption of Vesuvius, to save the lady with the gold rings and thus earn her love, had not heard a word of this gastronomic conversation. Only the two last words uttered by Max reached his ear, and as he had no desire to start a discussion, he made a motion of assent at random, and the amicable party walked back towards the inn, along the ramparts.

The table was set beneath the open porch, which served as a vestibule, and the white-washed walls of which were decorated with a number of daubs described by the host as the work of Salvator Rosa, Espagnolet, Massimo, and other famous names of the Neapolitan school, whom he felt called upon to extol.

"My venerable host," said Fabio, "do not display your eloquence to no purpose. We are not Englishmen, and we prefer young girls to old canvases. Better send us your wine-list by that handsome brunette with the velvety eyes, whom I saw in the hall."

The host, realising that they did not belong to the gullible class of Philistines and bourgeois, ceased to praise his picture-gallery and turned his attention to his cellar. In the first place he had all the wines of the best vintages: Château Margaux, Grand Laffite that had made a voyage to the Indies, Sillery de Moët, Hochmeyer, Scarlatti, port and porter, ale and ginger beer, white and red lacrymæ Christi, wine of Capri, and Falernian.

"What! you have Falernian, you villain, and you put it at the end of your list; you force us to listen to an intolerable œnological litany!" said Max, leaping at the innkeeper's throat with a gesture of comic rage; "why, have you no appreciation of local colour? are you altogether unworthy to live in this antique neighbourhood? But is your Falernian good? Was it put in amphoræ under the Consul Plancus—*Consule Planco?*"

"I don't know Plancus the Consul, and my wine isn't in amphoræ; but it's old and it cost ten carlines a bottle," replied the host.

The sun had set and night had fallen, a serene and transparent night, clearer, beyond question, than midday in London; the earth had an azure tint, and the sky silvery reflections of indescribable softness; the air was so calm that the flame of the candles on the table did not even flicker.

A young boy, playing the flute, approached the table and stood before the three guests, with his eyes fastened on them, in the attitude of a figure in a bas-relief, performing upon his sweet and melodious instrument one of those popular ballads, in a minor key, the charm of which is irresistible. It may be that that boy descended in a direct line from the flute-player who marched before Duilius.

"Our repast is set forth quite in antique style; all that we lack is some Gaditanian

dancing-girls and some wreaths of ivy,"
said Fabio, filling a large glass with Falernian.

"I feel in the mood for reciting Latin quo-
tations, like a *feuilleton* in the *Débats;* various
strophes of odes occur to me," said Max.

"Keep them to yourself," cried Octavian
and Fabio, justly alarmed; "nothing is so
indigestible as Latin at the table."

The conversation between young men, who,
cigars in mouth and elbows on the table, see
before them a number of empty bottles, especially when the wine is heady, is certain soon
to turn upon women. Each one set forth his
ideas, of which the following is a summary:

Fabio cared for nothing but beauty and
youth. Voluptuous and practical, he indulged
in no illusions and cherished no prejudices.
A peasant girl was as attractive to him as
a duchess, so long as she was lovely; the
body appealed to him more than the clothes;
he laughed heartily at certain of his friends
who were in love with a few yards of silk and
lace, and said that it would be more rational

to be enamoured of the show-window of a *marchand des nouveautés*. These opinions, which after all were very sensible and of which he made no secret, caused him to be looked upon as an eccentric man.

Max, who was less artistic than Fabio, cared only for difficult undertakings, complicated intrigues; he sought resistance to overcome, virtue to lead astray, and carried on a love affair like a game of chess, with moves long considered, effects held in suspense, surprises and stratagems worthy of Polybius. In the salon the woman who seemed to have the least liking for him was the one whom he would select as the object of his attacks; to force her to pass from aversion to love, by clever transitions, was to him a delicious pleasure; to impose himself upon hearts which spurned him, to master wills that fought against his ascendancy, seemed to him the most delightful of triumphs. Like some hunters, who scurry through fields and woods and valleys, in

rain and snow and sunshine, with excessive
fatigue and an ardour which nothing cools,
for a paltry quarry which in three cases out of
four they disdain to eat, Max, when he had
overtaken his victim, cared no more about
her, and would set out in quest of another
almost immediately.

As to Octavian, he confessed that reality
had little charm for him; not that he dreamed
a schoolboy's dreams, compounded of lilies
and roses, like one of Demoustier's madrigals;
but there were too many prosaic and unpleasant details about all beauty; too many doting,
decorated fathers; coquettish mothers, wearing natural flowers in false hair; ruddy-faced
cousins, meditating declarations of love; or
absurd aunts, in love with little dogs.   An
engraving in aquatint, after Horace Vernet or
Delaroche, hanging in a woman's bedroom,
was sufficient to arrest a nascent passion in
him.   Even more poetic than amorous, he re-
quired a terrace on Isola Bella, in Lake Maggiore, and a lovely moonlight night, as the

9   [129]

frame for an assignation. He would have liked to remove his love affair from the surroundings of ordinary life and transport its scene to the stars. So that he had been seized by an impossible and insane passion for all the great female types preserved by art or history, one after another. Like Faust, he had loved Helen; and he would have liked the undulations of the ages to bring to him one of those sublime incarnations of human desires and dreams, whose shape, invisible to vulgar eyes, continues to exist beyond Space and Time. He had formed for himself an imaginary harem, with Semiramis, Aspasia, Cleopatra, Diane de Poitiers, and Joanna of Aragon. Sometimes, too, he loved statues; and one day as he passed the *Venus of Milo* at the Louvre, he cried out: "Oh! who will restore your arms, to crush me against your marble breast?" In Rome the sight of a head of thick, braided hair, exhumed from an ancient tomb, had cast him into a strange ecstasy; he had tried, by means of two or three of the hairs, obtained by bribing the keeper, and placed in the hands of a somnambulist of great power, to evoke the shade and form of that woman; but the conducting fluid had evaporated after so many years, and the apparition had failed to come forth from everlasting darkness.

As Fabio had guessed, in front of the glass case in the Studj, the impression found in the cellar of Arrius Diomedes's villa caused in Octavian's mind insane outreachings towards a retrospective ideal; he tried to leave time and life behind him and to transport his soul to the age of Titus.

Max and Fabio retired to their apartment, and as their heads were a little heavy with the classic fumes of the Falernian, they speedily fell asleep. Octavian, who had often left his glass full before him, not wishing to disturb by vulgar intoxication the poetic drunkenness that was boiling in his brain, realised by the excited state of his nerves that sleep would not come to him; and he left the inn, walking slowly, to cool his brow and to calm his thoughts in the night air.

His feet unconsciously bore him to the gate through which one enters the dead city; he removed the wooden bar which closed the entrance and wandered about at random among the ruins.

The moon illuminated with its white light the pale houses, dividing the streets into two bands, of silvery light and bluish shadow. That nocturnal daylight, with its subdued tints, concealed the dilapidation of the buildings. One did not observe, as in the pitiless glare of the sun, the broken pillars, the house fronts riddled with cracks, the roofs crushed by the eruption; the lost parts were supplied by the half-light; and a sharp ray, like a touch of sentiment in a sketch for a picture, represented a whole crumbling edifice. The silent genii of the night seemed to have repaired the fossil city in preparation for some representation of an imaginary life.

At times Octavian fancied that he could see

vague human forms gliding in the shadow; but they vanished as soon as they reached the lighted spaces. A low whispering, an indefinite hum, floated through the silence. Our wanderer attributed this at first to the fluttering in his eyes, to a buzzing in his ears; or it might be an optical illusion, a sigh of the sea-breeze, or the flight of a lizard or a snake through the nettles; for everything lives in nature, even death; everything makes a noise, even silence. However, he was conscious of a sort of involuntary distress, a slight shudder, which might be caused by the cold night air, and which made his skin quiver. He turned his head twice or thrice; he no longer felt alone in the deserted city, as he had a moment before. Had his friends had the same idea as he, and were they looking for him among the ruins? Those shapes indistinctly seen, those vague footsteps,—were they Max and Fabio walking and chatting, and disappearing at the corner of a street? Octavian realised from his perturbation that that natural explanation was not true; and the reasoning which he mentally made on that subject did not convince him. The solitude and the shadow were peopled with invisible beings, whom he disturbed; he had fallen upon a mystery, and it seemed that they were waiting for him to go before beginning. Such were the extravagant ideas which passed through his brain, and which assumed much probability from the hour, the place, and a thousand alarming details, which those persons will understand who have been in some vast ruin at night.

As he passed a house which he had noticed during the day, and upon which the moon shone full, he saw, in absolutely perfect condition, a portico of which he had tried in the morning to restore the arrangement: four Doric columns, fluted half-way to the top, their shafts enveloped with a coat of red lead as with purple drapery, upheld a moulding with multicoloured ornamentation, which

the decorator seemed to have finished yesterday; on the wall beside the door a Laconian
molossus, painted in encaustic and accompanied by the familiar inscription, *Cave canem,*
barked at the moon and at visitors with pic-
tured fury. On the mosaic threshold the word
Have,[1] in Oscan and Latin characters, saluted
guests with its friendly syllables. The outer
walls, stained with ochre and red lead, had
not a crack. The house had been raised a
story, and the tiled roof, with bronze acroteria
placed at intervals, projected its profile un-
impaired against the light blue expanse of
the sky, in which there were a few pale
stars.

This extraordinary restoration, made between afternoon and evening by an unknown
architect, puzzled Octavian greatly; for he
was sure that he had seen that house in a de-
plorable state of dilapidation that same day.
The mysterious reconstructor had worked

---

[1] Welcome. The Osci were a people in Campania, whose
language closely resembled Latin.—[Trans.]

very rapidly, for the neighbouring houses had the same recent and new appearance; every pillar had its capital; not a stone, not a brick, not a pellicle of stucco, not a scale of paint was lacking on the gleaming façades; and through the openings of the peristyles, he could see about the marble basin of the *cavædium* pink and white laurels, myrtles, and pomegranates. All the historians were in error; the eruption had not taken place, or else the hand of time had retrograded twenty hours, of a century each, upon the dial of Eternity!

Octavian, surprised to the last degree, wondered whether he were sleeping on his feet and walking about in a dream. He questioned himself seriously to ascertain whether madness was waving its hallucinations before him; but he was forced to conclude that he was neither asleep nor insane.

A singular change had taken place in the atmosphere; vague rose-tints blended by violet gradations with the azure beams of the moon; the sky became lighter around the horizon; one would have said that the day was about to break. Octavian drew his watch; it marked midnight. Fearing that it had stopped, he pressed the repeating spring; the bell rang twelve times; it was surely midnight, and yet the light constantly increased, the moon faded away as the sky became more and more luminous. The sun rose!

Thereupon Octavian, in whose mind all ideas of time were hopelessly confused, was able to convince himself that he was walking, not in a dead Pompeii, the cold corpse of a city half removed from its winding-sheet, but in a living, young, intact Pompeii, over which the torrents of burning mud from Vesuvius had never flowed.

An inconceivable miracle had transported him, a Frenchman of the nineteenth century, back to the time of Titus, not in spirit, but in reality; or else had brought to him, from the depths of the past, a ruined city with its vanished people; for a man clothed in the ancient fashion came out of a house near by.

This man had short hair and a clean-shaven face, a brown tunic and a grayish cloak, the ends of which were caught up in such a way as not to impede his walk; he was walking rapidly, almost running, and passed Octavian close without seeing him. A basket made of spartum hung on his arm, and he bent his steps toward the Forum Nundinarium; he was a slave, some Davus,[1] going to market beyond a doubt.

Octavian heard the rumbling of wheels, and an ancient cart, drawn by white oxen and laden with vegetables, turned into the street. Beside the beasts walked a drover, with bare legs tanned by the sun, and sandal-shod feet, and clad in a sort of cotton shirt puffed out at the belt; a conical straw hat, fallen behind his back and held by a strap about his neck, allowed his face to be seen — a face of a type unknown to-day: the low forehead traversed by hard ridges, the hair black and curly, the

---

[1] A name frequently given to slaves in the comedies of Terence, etc.—[Trans.]

nose straight, the eyes as placid as those of his oxen, and a neck like that of a rustic Hercules. He gravely touched his beasts with the goad, with a statuesque pose that would have driven Ingres wild.

The drover saw Octavian and seemed surprised, but he kept on; he turned his head once, unable doubtless to understand the appearance of that personage who seemed so strange to him; but, in his tranquil, rustic stupidity, leaving the solution of the enigma to wiser folk.

Campanian peasants soon appeared, driving before them asses laden with skins of wine and tinkling their brazen bells; their faces differed from those of the peasants of to-day as a medallion does from a sou.

The city gradually became filled with people, like one of those panoramic pictures, uninhabited at first, which a change of the light enlivens with human beings hitherto invisible.

The nature of Octavian's sensations had changed. A moment before, in the deceptive shadows of the night, he had suffered from that discomfort which the bravest cannot avoid amid disquieting and abnormal circumstances which the reason cannot explain. His vague terror had changed to profound stupefaction; he could not doubt the testimony of his senses, their perception was so clear, and yet what he saw was absolutely incredible. Still unconvinced, he sought, by fixing his mind upon trivial but real details, to prove to himself that he was not the plaything of an hallucination. They were not phantoms who were passing before his eyes, for the bright light of the sun demonstrated their reality beyond question, and their shadows, lengthened by the morning light, were projected upon the pavements and the walls.

Unable to understand what was happening to him, Octavian, enchanted at heart to have one of his most cherished dreams come true, no longer fought against his adventure; he abandoned himself to all those marvellous happenings, without pretending to understand

them; he said to himself that since, by virtue
of some mysterious power, he was permitted
to live a few hours in an age long vanished,
he would not waste his time in seeking a
solution of an incomprehensible problem; and
he bravely walked on, gazing to right and to
left at the spectacle which was at once so old
and so new to him. But to what period in
the life of Pompeii had he been transported?
An ædile inscription engraved upon a wall
informed him, by the names of the officials
recorded, that it was the beginning of the
reign of Titus — about the year 79 of our era.
An idea suddenly passed through Octavian's
mind: the woman, the impression of whose
body he had admired at the museum at Naples,
must be alive, since the eruption of Vesuvius
in which she had perished had taken place
on the twenty-fourth of August in that very
year; and so he might find her, see her, speak
to her. The mad longing that he had felt at
the aspect of that lava moulded upon divine
outlines was perhaps to be gratified ; for

nothing could be impossible to a love which had had the power to make time go backward, and the same hour to pass twice through the hour-glass of Eternity.

While Octavian indulged in these reflections, lovely maidens went to the fountains, holding their urns steady on their heads with the ends of their white fingers; patricians in white togas bordered with bands of purple, followed by their procession of clients, bent their steps towards the Forum. Buyers crowded around the booths, all designated by carved and painted signs, and recalling by their small dimensions the Moorish booths in Algiers. Above most of these booths, a haughty phallus of coloured terra-cotta, and the inscription *Hic habitat Felicitas*, indicated superstitious precautions against the evil eye; Octavian even noticed one shop for the sale of amulets, the counter of which was covered with horns, forked branches of coral, and little figures of Priapus in gold, such as we find in Naples to-day, as a protection from the

jettatura; and he said to himself that a super-
stition outlives a religion.

As he followed the sidewalk which lines
each street in Pompeii, and thus deprives the
English of the credit of that convenient inven-
tion, Octavian found himself face to face with
a comely young man of about his own age,
dressed in a saffron-coloured tunic, with a
cloak of fine white linen, as soft as cashmere.
The aspect of Octavian, with his horrible
modern hat on his head, squeezed into a
scanty black coat, his legs confined in trousers,
and his feet pinched by shining boots, seemed
to surprise the young Pompeiian, as the sight
of an Iowa Indian or a Botocudo on Boulevard de Gand, with his feathers, his necklace
of bear's-paws, and his elaborate tattooing,
would surprise us. As he was a well-bred
young man, however, he did not burst out
laughing in Octavian's face, but taking pity
on that poor barbarian astray in that Græco-
Roman city, he said to him in a sweet, finely
modulated voice: " *Advena, salve!* "

Théophile Gautier

Nothing could be more natural than that a native of Pompeii under the reign of the divine Emperor Titus, most puissant and most august, should express himself in Latin; and yet Octavian shuddered when he heard that dead language in a living mouth. Then it was that he congratulated himself that he had been strong in Latin prose, and had won prizes in the general competition. The Latin taught at the university served him for the first time on this occasion, and recalling his class-room memories, he replied to the salute of the Pompeiian, after the style of *De Viris Illustribus* and *Selectæ e Profanis,* intelligibly enough, but with a Parisian accent which made the young man smile.

"Perhaps it would be easier for you to talk Greek," the Pompeiian said; "I am familiar with that language too, for I studied at Athens."

"I know even less Greek than Latin," replied Octavian; "I am from the country of the Gauls, from Paris, from Lutetia."

Arria Marcella

"I know that country. My grandfather served in Gaul under the great Julius Cæsar. But what a strange costume you wear! the Gauls whom I have seen at Rome were not thus attired."

Octavian attempted to make the young Pompeiian understand that twenty centuries had passed since the conquest of Gaul by Julius Cæsar, and that the fashions might well have changed; but he "lost his Latin," [1] and to tell the truth that was no great loss.

"My name is Rufus Holconius, and my house is yours," said the young man; "unless you prefer the freedom of the tavern; you can be very comfortable at the Inn of Albinus, near the gate of the suburb of Augustus Felix, or at the tavern of Sarinus, son of Publius, by the second tower; but if you wish, I will be your guide in this city, which is unfamiliar to you. Young barbarian, I am pleased with you, although you have tried to play on

---

[1] In French, an idiomatic phrase meaning to waste one's time, to take pains uselessly.—[Trans.]

my credulity by pretending that the Emperor
Titus, who reigns to-day, has been dead two
thousand years; and that the Nazarene, whose
villainous sectaries, smeared with pitch, have
illuminated Nero's gardens, now reigns alone
in the deserted sky, from which our mighty
gods have fallen.   By Pollux!" he added, as
he glanced at a red inscription at the corner
of a street, "you arrived in good time, for
Plautus's *Casina,* recently restored to the
stage, is to be acted to-day; it is a curious
and burlesque comedy, and will amuse you,
even if you understand only the pantomime.
Come with me; it is almost time for the play
to begin, and I will find you a place on the
benches allotted to guests and foreigners."

And Rufus Holconius walked in the direction of the small comic theatre which the
three friends had visited during the day.

The Frenchman and the citizen of Pompeii
walked through the Street of the Fountain
of Abundance and the Street of the Theatres,
passed the College and the Temple of Isis,

the Studio of the Sculptor, and entered the Odeon or Comic Theatre by a lateral passage. Thanks to the mediation of Holconius, Octavian obtained a seat near the proscenium, a place corresponding to our private boxes which front upon the stage. All eyes were immediately turned upon him with good-natured curiosity, and a low whispering ran about the amphitheatre.

The play had not yet begun; Octavian took advantage of that fact to look about the hall. The semicircular benches, terminating on each side in a magnificent lion's-paw carved in lava from Vesuvius, began at an empty space corresponding to our parterre, but much smaller, and paved with a mosaic of Greek marbles; each bench was thus longer than the one in front; a broader bench, at intervals, formed a distinct division, and four staircases corresponding to the four entrances, and ascending from the base to the top of the amphitheatre, divided it into five wedge-shaped portions broader at the top than at the bottom. The spectators, armed with their tickets, which consisted of little ivory blades on which were indicated by numbers the passage, the division, and the bench, with the title of the play to be performed and the name of its author, readily found their places. Magistrates, nobles, married men, young men, and soldiers with their gleaming bronze helmets, occupied benches by themselves. An admirable spectacle was presented by the beautiful togas, and great white cloaks, gracefully draped, displayed on the first benches, and forming a striking contrast with the varied costumes of the women, who sat above, and the gray cloaks of the common people, relegated to the uppermost benches, near the columns which supported the roof, and between which could be seen a sky of the deepest blue, like the azure field of the Panathenæa. A fine rain, scented with saffron, fell from the flies in imperceptible drops, and perfumed at the same time that it cooled the air. Octavian thought of the fetid emanations which vitiate the atmosphere of our theatres, which are so uncomfortable that one may regard them as places of torture; and he considered that civilisation had made little progress.

The curtain, supported by a transverse beam, disappeared in the depths of the orchestra; the musicians took their places in their gallery, and the Prologue appeared, in grotesque garb, with an uncouth masque fitted to his head like a helmet.

The Prologue, after saluting the audience and calling for applause, began a burlesque address:

"The old plays are like wine, which improves with age, and the *Casina,* dear to old men, should be no less so to the young; all may find amusement in it: some because they are familiar with it, others because they are not familiar with it. The play had been carefully remounted, and it should be listened to with the mind free from all anxiety, without a thought of debts or of creditors, for no one could be arrested in the theatre. It was a lucky day, the weather was fine, and the halcyons hovered over the Forum."

Then he gave an analysis of the comedy which the actors were about to present, with a minuteness of detail which proved that surprise counted for little in the pleasure which the ancients took in the theatre; he told how old Stalino, enamoured of his lovely slave Casina, wished to marry her to his farmer, Olympio, an obliging spouse, whose place he would take on the wedding night; and how Lycostrata, Stalino's wife, to thwart her vicious husband's lust, proposed to unite Casina to Chalinus, the esquire, with the idea of favouring her son's passion; and lastly how Stalino, completely deceived, mistook a young male slave, in disguise, for Casina, who, being recognised as free and of noble birth, marries her young master, whom she loves and by whom she is beloved.

The young Frenchman gazed absent-mind-

edly at the actors who, with their masques
with bronze mouths, laboured manfully on
the stage; the slaves ran hither and thither to
simulate zeal; the old man shook his head
and held out his trembling hands; the mother,
loud of speech, with a surly and disdainful
mien, strutted in her importance and quar-
relled with her husband, to the great amusement of the audience. All these characters
made their entrances and exits through three
doors in the wall at the rear, which com-
municated with the actors' greenroom. Stalino's house occupied one corner of the stage,
and that of his old friend Alcesimus was
opposite; this scenery, although very well
painted, represented rather the idea of a place
than the place itself, like most of the vague
scenery of the classic stage.

When the nuptial procession escorting the
false Casina came upon the stage, an immense
roar of laughter, like that which Homer
ascribes to the gods, arose from the benches
of the amphitheatre, and thunders of applause

woke the echoes of the enclosure; but Octavian had ceased to look or to listen.

On the benches allotted to the women, he had noticed a creature of marvellous beauty. At that moment, the lovely faces which had attracted his eyes disappeared like the stars before the dawn; everything vanished as in a dream; a mist blotted out the benches swarming with people, and the shrill voices of the actors seemed to die away in measureless distance.

He had received a sort of electric shock at the heart, and it seemed to him that sparks gushed from his breast when that woman's eyes turned towards him.

She was dark and pale; her wavy, curling hair, black as the tresses of Night, was raised slightly above the temples, after the Grecian fashion; and in her pallid face gleamed soft, melancholy eyes, laden with an indefinable expression of voluptuous sadness and passionate ennui; her mouth, disdainfully curled at the corners, protested by the living ardour of its

ruddy purple against the tranquil whiteness of
the masque; her neck presented those pure
and beautiful lines which are found to-day
only in statues. Her arms were bare to the
shoulders; and from the points of her superb
breasts, raising her dark red tunic, ran two
deep furrows which seemed to have been hollowed out of marble by Phidias or Cleomenes.

The sight of that bosom, so pure in its contour, so faultless in its curve, magnetically
affected Octavian; it seemed to him that those
rounded forms were perfectly adapted to the
impression at the museum at Naples, which
had cast him into such an impassioned reverie;
and a voice cried in the depths of his heart that
that woman was certainly the woman suffocated by the ashes from Vesuvius in the villa
of Arrius Diomedes. By what miracle did he
see her in life, attending the performance of
Casina? He did not try to understand; indeed, how was he there himself? He accepted
her presence as in a dream we accept the
intervention of persons long dead, who act

none the less with every appearance of life. Moreover, his excitement made reasoning impossible. For him the wheel of time had left its rut, and his victorious desire selected its place among the ages that had vanished. He found himself face to face with his chimera, one of the most intangible, a retrospective chimera. His life was filled to overflowing at a single stroke.

As he looked upon that face, so calm yet so impassioned, so cold yet so ardent, so dead yet so full of life, he realised that he had before him his first and his last love, his cup of supreme ecstasy; he felt the memories of all the women whom he had thought that he loved vanish like impalpable shadows, while his heart became void of every previous emotion. The past disappeared.

Meanwhile the fair Pompeiian, resting her chin on the palm of her hand, flashed at Octavian, while seeming to be intent upon the stage, a velvety glance from her nocturnal eyes, and that glance reached him as heavy and burning as a jet of molten lead. Then she leaned over and whispered in the ear of a girl who sat beside her.

The performance came to an end; the crowd poured out through the exits; Octavian, disdaining the services of his guide Holconius, rushed out through the first passage that presented itself. He had hardly reached the door when a hand rested on his arm, and a female voice said to him in an undertone, but in such wise that he did not lose a single word:

"I am Tyche Novoleia, purveyor to the pleasures of Arria Marcella, daughter of Arrius Diomedes; my mistress loves you; follow me."

Arria Marcella had entered her litter, which was borne by four muscular Syrian slaves, naked to the waist, whose bronze torsos gleamed like mirrors in the sunlight. The curtain of the litter was drawn aside, and a white hand, starred with rings, made a friendly sign to Octavian, as if to confirm the servant's words. The purple fold fell back and the litter moved away to the rhythmic step of the slaves.

Tyche led Octavian by a devious path; she crossed the streets, her feet barely touching the stones which joined the sidewalks and between which the wheels of the chariots rolled; she glided through the labyrinth with the unerring precision born of familiarity with the city. Octavian noticed that he was passing through those parts of Pompeii which recent investigations have not laid bare, and which were consequently unfamiliar to him. This strange circumstance among so many others did not surprise him. He had decided to be surprised by nothing. In all that archaic phantasmagoria, which would have driven an antiquary mad with joy, he saw naught but the deep, black eyes of Arria Marcella, and that superb bosom, triumphant over time, which even universal destruction had chosen to preserve.

They reached a secret door, which opened and closed instantly, and Octavian found himself in a courtyard surrounded by pillars of

Arria Marcella

Grecian marble of the Ionic order, painted half-way to the top a deep yellow colour, and with capitals decorated with red and blue reliefs; garlands of birthwort, with its broad green leaves, hung from the protuberances of the architecture, in the shape of a heart, like a natural arabesque; and beside a basin engirt with plants a red flamingo stood on one leg, a plume-flower among natural flowers.

The walls were decorated with frescoed panels, representing architectural fancies and imaginary landscapes. Octavian saw all these details with one swift glance, for Tyche delivered him into the hands of the slaves of the baths, who compelled his impatience to submit to all the refinements of the thermæ of the ancients. After passing through the different degrees of vapor-heat, after being tortured with the rough brush of the rubber, and deluged with cosmetics and perfumed oils, he was reclothed in a white tunic; he found at the other door Tyche, who took his hand and led him into another room elaborately decorated.

Théophile Gautier

On the ceiling were painted, with a marvellous perfection of design, a brilliancy of colouring, and a freedom of touch which denoted the great master and not the simple decorator, Mars, Venus, and Cupid; a frieze of deer, hares, and birds playing among the foliage surmounted a wainscoting of cipollino marble; the mosaic of the floor, a wonderful piece of work, executed perhaps by the hand of Sosimus of Pergamus, represented the remnants of a banquet, delineated with a skill that created a complete illusion.

At the end of the room, on a biclinium, or couch with two places, Arria Marcella reclined in a voluptuous and serene attitude, which recalled the reclining woman of Phidias, on the pediment of the Parthenon; her shoes, embroidered with pearls, lay at the foot of the couch, and her beautiful bare foot, purer and whiter than marble, peeped out beneath a light coverlet of byssus, which was thrown over her.

Earrings made in the shape of a pair of

balances, and bearing pearls in each scale,
trembled in the light beside her pale cheeks;
a necklace of gold balls, from which were
suspended pear-shaped brilliants, encircled
her breast, left partly bare by the carelessly
arranged folds of a straw-coloured peplum,
with a border of Grecian black; a black and
gold band gleamed amid her ebon hair, for
she had changed her costume since returning
from the theatre; and about her arm, like
the asp about the arm of Cleopatra, a gold
serpent, with jewels for eyes, was entwined,
and seemed to be trying to bite its tail.

A small table, with griffins for feet, inlaid
with mother-of-pearl, silver, and ivory, stood
beside the bed, laden with divers delicacies
served in dishes of silver and gold and earth-
enware, enamelled with beautiful paintings.
There was a Phasian bird, lying in its feathers,
and different fruits which their varying seasons
make it seldom possible to serve at the same
time.

Everything seemed to indicate that a guest

was expected; the floor was strewn with fresh flowers, and the amphoræ of wine were plunged in urns filled with snow.

Arria Marcella motioned to Octavian to recline beside her on the biclinium and to share her repast; the young man, half-mad with surprise and love, took at random a mouthful or two of the dishes handed to him by small Asiatic slaves with curled hair and short tunics. Arria did not eat; but she frequently put to her lips a myrrhine glass of an opaline tint, filled with wine of a dark purple colour like thickened blood; as she drank, an imperceptible flush rose to her pale cheeks from her heart, which had not beaten for so many years; but her bare arm, which Octavian touched as he raised his cup, was cold as the skin of a serpent or the marble of a tomb.

"Ah! when you paused in the Studj to gaze upon the bit of hardened clay which retains my figure," said Arria Marcella, fastening her long, liquid glance upon Octavian, "and your thoughts rushed ardently out towards me, my heart was conscious of it in that world where I soar, invisible to vulgar eyes; faith makes the god and love the woman; one is not really dead except when one is no longer loved; your desire restored me to life, the potent evocation of your heart annihilated the distance which lay between us."

This idea of the evocation of love, expressed by the young woman, coincided with Octavian's philosophical beliefs — beliefs which we are not far from sharing.

In fact, nothing dies; everything exists forever; no power can annihilate that which once had being. Every act, every word, every form, every thought that falls into the universal ocean of things produces circles there, which go on widening and widening to the confines of eternity. Material shape disappears only from the ordinary eyes, and the spectres which are detached from it people infinity. Paris continues to abduct Helen in some unknown region of space. Cleopatra's galley swells its silken sails over the azure surface of an ideal Cydnus. Some impassioned and powerful minds have been able to bring back ages that seem to have vanished, and to restore to life persons dead to all others. Faust had for his mistress the daughter of Tyndarus, and carried her to his Gothic castle from the mysterious abysses of Hades. Octavian had lived a single day in the reign of Titus and had won the love of Arria Marcella, daughter of Arrius Diomedes, who at that moment was reclining by his side upon an antique couch, in a city that for all the rest of the world had ceased to exist.

"By my distaste for other women," replied Octavian, "by my unconquerable tendency to dream, which lured me towards the radiant shapes in the desert of past ages, like alluring stars, I realised that I should never love except apart from Time and Space. It was you whom I awaited, and that fragile vestige preserved by the curiosity of men placed me in relations with your heart by its hidden magnetism. I know not whether you are a dream or a reality, a phantom or a woman; whether like Ixion I am pressing a cloud to my deluded breast, or whether I am the plaything of some vile witchcraft; but this I do know, that you will be my first and my last love."

"May Cupid, son of Venus, hear your promise!" said Arria Marcella, resting her head upon the shoulder of her lover, who threw his arms about her in a passionate embrace. "Oh! press me to your young breast, envelop me with your warm breath; I am cold because I have remained so long without love." And Octavian felt against his heart the rise and fall of that beautiful bosom, the mould of which he had admired that very morning through the glass of a case in the museum; the coolness of that beautiful flesh penetrated him through his tunic and made him burn. The gold and black band had become detached from Arria's head, as it was passionately thrown back, and her hair spread like a black wave over the purple pillow.

The slaves had removed the table. Naught could be heard save a confused sound of kisses and sighs. The pet quails, heedless of that amorous scene, picked from the mosaic pavement the crumbs of the repast, uttering little cries.

Suddenly the brazen rings of the portière at the door of the room moved on their rod, and an aged man of stern aspect, draped in an ample brown cloak, appeared in the door-way. His gray beard was divided into two points like those of the Nazarenes, and his face was furrowed as by the fatigue of penances; a small crucifix of black wood hung from his neck, and left no doubt as to his faith: he belonged to the sect, then of recent birth, of the Disciples of the Christ.

At sight of him, Arria Marcella, overwhelmed with confusion, concealed her face beneath the folds of her cloak, like a bird

that puts its head under its wing before an
enemy whom it cannot escape, to spare itself at least the horror of looking upon him;
while Octavian, rising on his elbow, gazed
fixedly at the unwelcome intruder who thus
abruptly interrupted his happiness.

"Arria, Arria," said the stern-faced man
in a tone of reproach, " was not the time that
thou livedst sufficient for thine evil behaviour,
and must thine infamous amours encroach
upon the centuries to which they do not belong? Canst thou not leave the living in
their sphere? have not thine ashes grown
cold since the day when thou didst die un-
repentant beneath the fiery rain from the
volcano? Have not two thousand years of
death calmed thine ardour, and do thy devour-
ing arms still draw to thy marble breast,
devoid of heart, the poor fools intoxicated by
thy philtres?"

"I pray thee, Arrius, my father, do not
upbraid me in the name of that morose religion which was never mine; for my part,

I believe in our ancient gods, who love life, youth, beauty, and pleasure; do not force me back into colourless oblivion. Let me enjoy this existence which love has restored to me."

"Hold thy peace, impious girl; talk not to me of thy gods, who are demons. Let this young man, fettered by thine impure seductions, go his way; seek no longer to lure him out of the circle of life which God has meted out to him; return to the limbo of paganism with thine Asiatic, Roman, or Greek lovers. Young Christian, abandon this worm, which would seem to thee more hidious than Empusa and Phorkys, couldst thou but see her as she really is."

Octavian, deathly pale, frozen with horror, tried to speak; but his voice clung to his throat, as Virgil would say.

"Wilt thou obey me, Arria?" cried the tall man, imperatively.

"No, never!" replied Arria, with gleaming eyes, as she encircled Octavian in her lovely, statuesque arms, as cold, and hard, and rigid as marble. Her frenzied beauty, enhanced by the conflict, shone forth at that supreme moment with supernatural brightness, as if to leave with her young lover an imperishable memory.

"In that case, unhappy creature," rejoined the old man, "we must employ strong methods, and render your nothingness palpable and visible to this deluded child"; and in a voice vibrating with authority he uttered a formula of exorcism, which caused the purple hues which the black wine from the myrrhine glass had brought to Arria's cheeks to fade away.

At that moment, the distant bell of one of the hamlets in the recesses of the mountain, pealed forth the first notes of the angelic salutation.

At that sound a long-drawn sigh of agony issued from the young woman's broken heart. Octavian felt the arms which embraced him release their hold; the draperies which covered her sank together, as if the frame which held them up had collapsed, and the unhappy midnight wanderer saw beside him upon the banquet-couch only a pinch of ashes mingled with a few calcined bones, among which glittered golden bracelets and jewels, and shapeless remains, such probably as were discovered on disinterring the house of Arrius Diomedes.

He uttered a terrible cry and lost consciousness.

The old man had disappeared. The sun rose, and the apartment, so sumptuously decorated but now, was naught but a dismantled ruin.

After sleeping heavily because of the libations of the preceding night, Max and Fabio suddenly awoke, and their first thought was to call their comrade, whose room was near theirs, with one of those jocose calls which travellers sometimes make use of; Octavian, for a very good reason, did not reply. Fabio and Max, receiving no answer, entered their friend's room and found that the bed had not been disturbed.

"He must have fallen asleep in a chair," said Fabio, "unable to reach his bed; for dear Octavian's head is n't very strong; and he probably went out early to dissipate the fumes of the wine in the fresh morning air."

"But he drank very little," said Max, musingly. "It seems to me very strange. Let us go and look for him."

The two friends, assisted by the guide, went through all the streets and squares and lanes of Pompeii, entered all the interesting houses, where they imagined that Octavian might be engaged in copying a picture or taking down an inscription, and finally found him in a swoon upon the disjoined mosaic floor of a small half-ruined room. They had much difficulty in restoring him to life, and when he recovered consciousness, he vouchsafed no other explanation than that it had occurred to him to see Pompeii by moonlight, and that he had been seized with a sudden faintness, which probably would have no serious consequences.

The little party returned to Naples by the railway, as they had come; and that evening, in their box at the San Carlo, Max and Fabio, with the aid of their opera-glasses, watched a swarm of nymphs hopping about in a ballet, under the lead of Amalia Ferraris, the *danseuse* then in vogue, all dressed in frightful green tights, which made them look like grasshoppers stung by a tarantula. Octavian, pale, with wandering eyes and the bearing of one crushed by grief, seemed to have no idea of what was taking place on the stage, so difficult was it for him to recover the sentiment of real life, after the marvellous adventures of the night.

After that visit to Pompeii, Octavian fell into a dismal melancholy, which the merry humour or the jests of his companions aggravated rather than soothed; the image of Arria Marcella pursued him constantly, and the sad termination of his fantastic intrigue did not destroy its charm.

Unable to endure it any longer, he returned secretly to Pompeii, and walked about, as on the first occasion, among the ruins by moonlight, his heart throbbing with an insane hope; but the hallucination was not repeated, he saw nothing but lizards scuttling over the stones; he heard only the screams of the frightened night-birds; he did not meet again his friend Rufus Holconius; Tyche did not come to him and place her slender hand on his arm; Arria Marcella obstinately slumbered in her dust.

In despair, Octavian finally married a young and charming Englishwoman, who is madly in love with him. His treatment of his wife is unexceptionable; and yet Ellen, with that instinct of the heart which nothing deceives, feels that her husband is enamoured of another; —but of whom? That is something which the closest watching has not succeeded in discovering. Octavian keeps no ballet-dancer; in society he addresses only commonplace compliments to women; he even responded

very coolly to the overtures of a Russian princess, celebrated for her beauty and her coquetry. A secret drawer, opened during her
husband's absence, furnished no proof of infidelity to feed Ellen's suspicions. But how
could it occur to her to be jealous of Arria
Marcella, daughter of Arrius Diomedes, the
freedman of Tiberius ?

1852.

The Dead Leman

The Dead Leman

YOU ask me, brother, if I have ever loved; yes. It is a strange and terrible story, and although I am sixty-six years old, I hardly dare to stir the ashes of that memory. I am unwilling to refuse you anything, but I would not tell such a tale to a mind less experienced than yours. The incidents are so extraordinary that I cannot believe that they ever happened to me. For more than three years I was the sport of a strange and devilish delusion. I, a poor country priest, led the life of one damned, the life of a worldling, of a Sardanapalus, every night in dreams (God grant they were dreams!). One single look too freely cast upon a woman nearly caused the ruin of my soul; but at last, with the aid of God and of my blessed patron saint, I succeeded in expelling the wicked spirit which had taken possession of me. My life was intermingled with a nocturnal life entirely different. By day I was a priest of the Lord, chaste, intent upon prayer and sacred things; at night, as soon as I had closed my eyes, I became a young nobleman, a fine connoisseur in women, dogs, and horses, throwing dice, drinking, and blaspheming; and when I woke at sunrise, it seemed to me that, on the other hand, I had fallen asleep, and that I was dreaming that I was a priest. My mind has retained memories, objects, and words of that somnambulistic life, from which I cannot escape, and although I have never gone without the bounds of my presbytery, one would say, to hear me, that I was a man who, having become satiated with everything and having turned his back upon the world, had betaken himself to religion, and proposed to end his too agitated life in the bosom of God, rather than a humble seminarist, who had grown old in this obscure curacy, in the depths of the woods, and aloof from all connection with the affairs of his time.

The Dead Leman

Yes, I loved as no one in the world has ever loved, with an insensate and furious passion, so violent that I am surprised that it did not cause my heart to burst. Ah! what nights! what nights!

From my earliest childhood, I had felt a calling to the priesthood; so that all my studies tended in that direction, and my life, up to the age of twenty-four, was simply a prolonged novitiate. My theological studies completed, I passed through all the minor orders in succession, and my superiors deemed me worthy, despite my extreme youth, to take the last and formidable step. The day of my ordination was fixed for Easter week.

I had never been into society; for me the world was the enclosure of the college and the seminary. I had a vague knowledge that there was a something called woman, but I never dwelt upon the subject; I was absolutely innocent. I saw my infirm old mother only twice a year; that was the extent of my connection with the outside world.

I had no regrets, I felt not the slightest hesitation in the face of that irrevocable engagement; I was overflowing with joy and impatience. Never did a young fiancé count the hours with more feverish ardour; I did not sleep, I dreamed that I was saying mass; I could imagine nothing nobler in the world than to be a priest; I would have declined to be a king or a poet. My ambition could conceive of no loftier aim.

I say this to show you that the things that happened to me should not have happened, and how inexplicable was the fascination to which I fell a victim.

When the great day came, I walked to the church with a step so light that it seemed to me that I was sustained in air, or that I had wings on my shoulders. I fancied myself an angel, and I was amazed at the gloomy and preoccupied faces of my companions; for there were several of us. I had passed the night in prayer, and I was in a condition almost bordering on ecstacy. The bishop, a venerable old man, seemed to me to be God the Father leaning over His eternity, and I beheld Heaven through the arched ceiling of the temple.

You know the details of the ceremony: the benediction, the communion under both forms, the anointing of the palms of the hands with the novice's oil, and lastly the holy sacrifice, administered by the priest in conjunction with the bishop. I will not dwell upon it. Oh! how truly did Job say that he is imprudent who does not conclude a covenant with his eyes! I chanced to raise my head, which I had thus far kept lowered, and I saw before me, so near that it seemed I could have touched her, although in reality she was at a considerable distance and on the other side of the rail, a young woman of rare beauty, attired with royal magnificence. It was as if scales fell from my eyes. I experienced the sensation of a blind man suddenly recovering his sight. The bishop, but now so radiant, suddenly faded away, the candles turned pale in their golden sconces, like stars at dawn, and the whole church was enveloped in complete darkness. The charming creature stood out against that dark background like an angelic revelation; she seemed illuminated by herself, and to shed light rather than to receive it.

I lowered my eyes, fully determined not to raise them again, in order to escape the influence of exterior objects; for distraction took more and more complete possession of me, and I hardly knew what I was doing.

A moment later I opened my eyes again, for through my lashes I could see her glistening with all the colours of the rainbow, and in a purplish penumbra as when one looks at the sun.

Oh! how lovely she was! The greatest painters, when, turning to Heaven for ideal beauty, they have brought to earth the divine portrait of the Madonna, do not even approach that wondrous reality. Neither the verses of the poet nor the painter's palette can convey an idea of it. She was rather tall, with the

form and bearing of a goddess; her hair, of
a soft, light shade, was parted on top of her
head, and fell over her temples like two
golden waves; she was like a queen with her
diadem; her forehead, of a bluish and transparent whiteness, rose broad and serene over
arched eyebrows, almost black; a peculiarity
which intensified the effect of sea-green pupils
of an unsustainable vivacity and brilliancy.
What eyes! With one flash they decided
a man's destiny; they had a limpidity, a life,
an ardour, a glistening humidity which I
have never seen in other human eyes; they
shot forth rays like arrows, which I distinctly saw flying towards my heart. I do not
know whether the flame which illuminated
them came from heaven or hell, but it surely
came from one or the other. That woman
was an angel or a demon, perhaps both; she
certainly did not issue from the loins of Eve,
our common mother. Teeth of the purest
pearl sparkled in her ruddy smile, and little
dimples appeared with each motion of her

mouth, in the satiny rose of her adorable cheeks. As for her nostrils, they were regal in their graceful and dignified shape, and indicated the noblest origin. A lustre as of agate played upon the smooth, glossy skin of her half-bare shoulders, and strings of great blonde pearls, of a shade almost like her neck, hung down upon her bosom. From time to time she elevated her head with the undulating grace of a snake, or of a startled peacock, and imparted a slight quiver to the high embroidered openwork ruff which surrounded her neck like a silver trelliswork.

She wore a dress of flame-coloured velvet, and from the broad sleeves lined with ermine peeped forth patrician hands of infinite delicacy, with long, plump fingers, and so transparent that they allowed the light to shine through, like Aurora's.

All these details are still vivid as if they were of yesterday, and although I was extremely perturbed, nothing escaped me: the faintest touch of shading, the little dark spot at the point of the chin, the imperceptible down at the parting of the lips, the velvety softness of the forehead, the quivering shadow of the eyelashes on the cheeks, I grasped them all with amazing lucidity.

As I gazed at her, I felt doors open within me which had hitherto been closed; the rubbish was cleared away from choked-up openings on every side, and gave me a glimpse of prospects theretofore undreamed of; life appeared to me in a totally different aspect; I was born to a new order of ideas. A frightful anguish gnawed at my heart; every moment that passed seemed to me but a second and yet a century. The ceremony progressed, however, and I was carried very far from the world, the entrance to which my rising passions fiercely besieged. I said yes, however, when I longed to say no; when everything within me rose in revolt and protest against the violence my tongue exerted on my mind; a hidden force tore the words from my throat against my will. It is the same feeling, perhaps, that makes so many maidens go to the altar with the firm resolution of refusing publicly the husband who is forced upon them, although not a single one fulfils her intention. It is that, without doubt, which makes so many unhappy novices take the veil, although they are firmly resolved to tear it in shreds when the time comes to pronounce their vows. One dares not cause such a scandal before the world, or disappoint the expectation of so many people; all their wishes, all their glances seem to weigh upon you like a cloak of lead; and then, measures are so carefully taken, everything is so fully arranged beforehand, in so clearly irrevocable a fashion, that the will yields to the weight of the thing and collapses utterly.

The expression of the fair unknown changed as the ceremony progressed. Tender and caressing at first, it became disdainful and dissatisfied, as if because it had not been understood.

I made an effort that might have moved a

The Dead Leman

mountain, to cry out that I would not be a priest; but I could not accomplish it; my tongue was glued to my palate, and it was impossible for me to give effect to my desire by the least syllable of negation. Fully awake as I was, I was in a plight similar to that stage of a nightmare where you try to utter a word upon which your life depends, but cannot succeed.

She seemed to appreciate the martyrdom I was suffering, and, as if to encourage me, she flashed at me a glance replete with divine promise. Her eyes were a poem of which each glance formed a stanza.

She seemed to say to me:

"If thou wilt be mine, I will make thee happier than God Himself in His Paradise; the very angels will be jealous of thee. Tear away that funereal shroud in which thou art about to wrap thyself; I am Beauty, I am Youth, I am Life; come to me and together we shall be Love. What can Jehovah offer you in exchange? Our lives will flow on like a dream, and will be but an everlasting kiss. Pour the wine from that chalice, and thou art free. I will bear thee away to unknown isles; thou shalt sleep between my breasts, in a bed of massy gold, beneath a canopy of silver; for I love thee and I long to take thee away from this God of thine, before whom so many noble hearts pour out floods of love which never reach Him."

It seemed to me that I could hear these words, uttered in a rhythm of infinite sweetness; for her glance was actually sonorous, and the sentences that her eyes sent forth to me echoed in the depths of my heart as if an invisible mouth had breathed them into my very being. I felt that I was ready to renounce God, and yet my heart mechanically went through with the formalities of the ceremony. The beautiful creature cast at me a second glance, so beseeching, so despairing, that keen blades pierced my heart, and I felt more sword-points in my breast than Our Lady of Sorrows herself.

The Dead Leman

All was consummated; I had become a priest.

Never did human features express such poignant suffering; the maiden who sees her betrothed suddenly fall dead at her side, the mother by her child's empty cradle, Eve seated at the threshold of the gate of Paradise, the miser who finds a stone in place of his hoard, the poet who has allowed the only copy of the manuscript of his finest work to fall into the fire, seem no more crushed and inconsolable. The blood entirely left her charming face, and she became as white as marble; her beautiful arms fell beside her body, as if the muscles had lost their power; and she leaned against a pillar, for her limbs trembled and gave way beneath her. As for myself, with livid cheeks and brow bathed in sweat more bloody than that of Calvary, I walked with tottering steps towards the door of the church; I was suffocating; the arches seemed to rest on my shoulders, and I fancied that my head alone bore the whole weight of the dome.

Théophile Gautier

As I was about to cross the threshold, a hand suddenly seized mine, a woman's hand! I had never touched one before. It was as cold as the skin of a serpent, and yet the impression burned like the brand of a red-hot iron. It was she. "Unhappy man! unhappy man! what hast thou done?" she said in a low voice; then she disappeared in the crowd.

The aged bishop passed; he looked at me with a stern expression. I cut the most extraordinary figure imaginable; I turned pale, I flushed, I was giddy. One of my comrades had pity on me, and led me away; I was incapable of finding the road to the seminary alone. At the corner of the street, while the young priest's head was turned in another direction, a negro page, singularly attired, approached me and placed in my hand, without stopping, a small wallet with corners of carved gold, motioning to me to hide it; I slipped it up my sleeve and kept it there until I was alone in my cell. Then I broke the lock;

there was nothing inside save two sheets of paper with the words: "Clarimonde, at the Concini Palace." I was then so little acquainted with the affairs of life that I knew nothing of Clarimonde despite her celebrity, and I was absolutely ignorant as to the location of the Concini Palace. I made a thousand conjectures, each more extravagant than the last; but in truth, provided that I might see her again, I cared very little what she might be, whether a great lady or a courtesan.

That passion, born in an instant, had taken imperishable root; I did not even think of trying to tear it up, I realised so fully that it was impossible. That woman had taken complete possession of me; a single glance had sufficed to change me; she had breathed her will into me; I no longer lived in myself, but in her and through her. I did a thousand foolish things; I kissed the spot on my hand that she had touched, and I repeated her name hours at a time. I had only to close my eyes to see her as distinctly as if she were really

present, and I said to myself again and again
the words that she had said to me beneath
the church porch: "Unhappy man! unhappy
man! what hast thou done?" I realised all
the horror of my situation, and the terrible
and fatal aspects of the profession I had embraced were clearly revealed to me. To be
a priest! That is to say, to be chaste, not to
love, to distinguish neither sex nor age, to
turn aside from all beauty, to put out one's
eyes, to crawl beneath the icy shadow of a
cloister or a church, to see none but the
dying, to keep vigil by unknown corpses,
and to wear mourning for yourself over your
black soutane, so that your garment may be
used to make your winding-sheet!

And I felt life rising within me like a sub-
terranean lake expanding and overflowing;
my blood beat violently in my veins; my
youth, so long held in restraint, suddenly
burst forth like the aloe which takes a hundred years to flower and then blossoms with
a clap of thunder.

The Dead Leman

How was I to arrange to see Clarimonde again? I had no pretext for leaving the seminary, as I knew no one in the city; indeed, I was not to remain there, and I was waiting only until I should be told what curacy I was to occupy. I tried to loosen the bars at the window; but it was terribly high, and as I had no ladder, I could not think of escaping that way. Besides, I could descend only at night; and how could I find my way through the inextricable labyrinth of streets? All these obstacles, which would have been nothing at all to others, were enormous to me, a poor seminarist, in love since yesterday, without experience, without money, and without attire.

"Ah! if I had not been a priest, I might have seen her every day; I might have been her lover, her husband," I said to myself in my blindness; "instead of being wrapped in my dismal winding-sheet, I should have garments of silk and velvet, gold chains, a sword, and plumes, like the gallant young cavaliers.

My hair, instead of being dishonoured by a broad tonsure, would play about my neck in waving curls; I should have a fine waxed mustache, I should be a hero." But an hour passed in front of an altar, a few words barely spoken, had cut me off forever from the ranks of the living, and I myself had sealed the door of my tomb; I had shot with my own hand the bolt of my prison!

I stood at the window. The sky was beautifully blue, the trees had donned their spring robes; Nature bedecked herself with ironical joy. The square was full of people, going and coming; young beaux and youthful beauties, two by two, walked towards the garden and the arbours. Merry companions passed, singing drinking-songs; there was a bustle, an animation, a merriment, which made my black garments and my solitude stand out in painful relief. A young mother, on her doorstep, was playing with her child; she kissed its little red lips, still empearled with drops of milk, and indulged in a thousand of those divine puerilities which mothers alone can invent. The father, standing at a little distance, smiled pleasantly at the charming group, and his folded arms pressed his joy to his heart. I could not endure that spectacle; I closed my window and threw myself on my bed with a horrible hatred and jealousy in my heart, gnawing my fingers and my bedclothes like a tiger who has fasted three days.

I do not know how long I remained in this condition; but as I turned over in a spasm of frenzy, I saw the Abbé Sérapion standing in the middle of the room and watching me closely. I was ashamed of myself, and dropping my head upon my breast, covered my eyes with my hand.

" Romuald, my friend, something extraordinary is taking place in you," said Sérapion after a few moments of silence; " your conduct is really inexplicable! You, who were so pious, so quiet, and so gentle, rave in your cell like a wild beast. Beware, my brother, and do not listen to the suggestions of the devil; the evil spirit, irritated because you have consecrated yourself forever to the Lord, is prowling about you like a savage wolf, making a last effort to lure you to him. Instead of allowing yourself to be vanquished, my dear Romuald, make a shield for yourself with prayers, a buckler with mortifications, and fight valiantly against the foe; you will overcome him. Trial is necessary to virtue, and gold comes forth refined from the crucible. Do not be dismayed or discouraged; the most watchful and steadfast souls have had such moments. Pray, fast, meditate, and the evil spirit will depart."

The Abbé Sérapion's words caused me to reflect, and I became a little calmer.

"I came to inform you of your appointment to the curacy of C——. The priest who held it has died, and monseigneur the bishop has instructed me to go with you and install you; be ready to-morrow."

I answered with a nod that I would be,

and the abbé withdrew. I opened my missal and began to read prayers; but the lines soon became blurred beneath my eyes; the thread of the ideas became entangled in my brain, and the book slipped from my hands unheeded.

To go away on the morrow without seeing her again! To add still another impossibility to those which already lay between us! To lose forever the hope of meeting her, unless by a miracle! Write to her?—by whom could I send my letter? With the sacred character which I bore, to whom could I open my heart, in whom could I confide? I was terribly perplexed. And then, what Abbé Sérapion had said to me of the wiles of the devil returned to my mind; the oddity of the adventure, the supernatural beauty of Clarimonde, the phosphorescent gleam of her eyes, the burning touch of her hand, the confusion into which she had thrown me, the sudden change which had taken place in me, my piety vanished in an instant —all these clearly demonstrated the presence of the devil, and perhaps that satiny hand was only the glove with which he had covered his claw. These ideas caused me the greatest alarm; I picked up the missal which had fallen from my knees to the floor, and began anew to pray.

The next day Sérapion called for me; two mules awaited us at the door, laden with our thin valises; he mounted one and I the other as well as we might. As we rode through the streets of the city, I looked at all the windows and all the balconies to see if I could not espy Clarimonde; but it was too early, the city had not yet opened its eyes. My glance tried to pierce behind the blinds and through the curtains of all the palaces we passed. Sérapion doubtless attributed my curiosity to the beauty of the architecture, for he slackened the pace of his steed to give me time to look. At last we reached the city gates and began to climb the hill. When I was at the top, I turned to glance once more

The Dead Leman

at the place where Clarimonde lived. The shadow of a cloud covered the city entirely; its blue and red roofs were blended in the prevailing half-light, above which rose here and there, like patches of white foam, the morning smoke. By a curious optical effect, a single edifice surpassing in height the neighbouring buildings, which were completely drowned in vapour, stood out, golden-hued, in a single beam of light; although it was more than a league away, it seemed very near. I could distinguish the slightest details, the turrets, the platforms, the windows, and even the weather-vanes in the shape of a swallow's tail.

"What is the palace that I see yonder, all lighted up by the sun?" I asked Sérapion. He put his hand over his eyes, and, having looked, he answered:

"It is the ancient palace which Prince Concini has given to the courtesan Clarimonde; shocking scenes take place there."

At that moment—and I do not know even

now whether it was a reality or an illusion
—I fancied that I saw a slender white form
glide along the terrace, gleam for an instant,
and vanish. It was Clarimonde!

Oh! did she know that at that moment,
from the height of the rugged road which
separated me from her, and which I was
never to descend again, I was gazing, ardent
and restless, at the palace in which she dwelt,
and which a mocking trick of the light seemed
to bring nearer to me, as if to invite me to
enter as its lord? Doubtless she knew it, and
her soul was too closely bound to mine not
to feel its slightest emotions; and it was
that sympathy which had impelled her, still
clad in her night-robe, to go out upon the
terrace amid the icy dews of the morning.

The shadow gained the palace, and there
was nothing but a motionless ocean of roofs
and gables, in which one could distinguish
naught save one mountainous undulation. Sérapion urged forward his mule, whose gait
mine immediately imitated, and a turn in the

road concealed from me forever the city of
S——; for I was destined never to go thither
again. After travelling three days through an
unattractive country, we saw the weather-vane
of the steeple of the church in which I was
to officiate appear through the trees; and after
riding through a number of winding streets,
lined with hovels and garden-plots, we found
ourselves in front of the edifice, which was
not very magnificent. A porch ornamented
with a moulding or two, and two or three
pillars of rough-hewn sandstone, a tile roof,
and buttresses of the same material as the
pillars—that was all. At the left was the
cemetery, full of high weeds, with a tall iron
cross in the centre; at the right, and in the
shadow of the church, the presbytery. It was
a house of extreme simplicity, clean, but bare.
We entered; a few hens were pecking at
grains of oats scattered on the ground; accustomed apparently to the black garments of
ecclesiastics, they did not take fright at our
presence and hardly moved aside to let us

pass. We heard a hoarse, wheezy bark, and an old dog ran towards us. It was my predecessor's dog. He had the dull eye, the gray hair, and all the other symptoms of the extremest old age which a dog may attain. I patted him gently with my hand and he at once walked beside me with an air of inexpressible gratification. A woman advanced in years, who had been the former curé's housekeeper, also came to meet us, and after showing me into a room on the ground floor, asked me if I intended to keep her. I told her that I would retain her and the dog, the hens, too, and all the furniture which her master had left her at his death; this caused her a transport of joy, and the Abbé Sérapion at once gave her the price that she asked.

My installation completed, the Abbé Sérapion returned to the seminary. So I was left alone, with nobody to lean upon but myself. Thoughts of Clarimonde began to haunt me once more, and strive as I would to banish them, I could not always succeed. One even-

The Dead Leman

ing, as I walked along the box-bordered paths
of my little garden, it seemed to me that I saw
through the hedge a female form following
my every movement, and sea-green eyes
gleaming among the leaves; but it was only
an illusion, and, having gone to the other side
of the hedge, I found nothing there but a foot-
print on the gravel, so small that one would
have said that it was made by a child's foot.
The garden was enclosed by very high
walls; I searched every nook and corner, and
there was no one there. I have never been
able to explain that circumstance, which,
however, was as nothing compared with the
strange things which were to happen to me.

I had been living thus a year, performing
with scrupulous exactitude all the duties of
my profession, praying, fasting, exhorting, and
assisting the sick, and giving alms to such an
extent that I went without the most indispensable necessities of life. But I was conscious of a great aridness within me, and
the sources of grace were closed to me. I

enjoyed none of that happiness which the accomplishment of a sacred mission affords; my thoughts were elsewhere, and Clarimonde's words often came to my lips like a sort of involuntary refrain. O brother, consider this well! Because I raised my eyes a single time to a woman's face, for a fault apparently so venial, I experienced for many years the most wretched perturbation of spirit, and the happiness of my life was forever destroyed.

I will dwell no longer upon these defeats and these inward victories always followed by heavier falls, but I will pass at once to a decisive incident. One night some one rang violently at my door. The aged housekeeper answered the bell, and a copper-coloured man, richly clad, but in outlandish fashion, and wearing a long dagger, appeared in the rays of Barbara's lantern. Her first impulse was one of terror; but the man reassured her and told her that he must see me at once about a matter concerning my ministry. Barbara showed him upstairs, where I was on the point of retiring. The man told me that his mistress, a very great lady, was at death's door and desired to see a priest. I replied that I was ready to accompany him; I took with me what I needed for administering extreme unction, and I went downstairs in all haste. At the door two horses black as night were pawing the ground impatiently and blowing from their nostrils long streams of vapour against their breasts. He held the stirrup for me and assisted me to mount one of them; then he leaped upon the other, simply placing one hand upon the pommel of the saddle. He pressed his knees against the horse's flanks and dropped the reins; the beast started off like an arrow. Mine, whose bridle he held, also fell into a gallop and kept pace with him. We devoured the road; the ground glided away beneath our feet, gray and streaked; and the black silhouettes of the trees fled like an army in full retreat. We passed through a forest so intensely dark and so icy chill that I felt a shudder of superstitious terror run through my body. The sparks that our horses' shoes struck upon the stones left a trail of fire as it were behind us as we passed; and if any one had seen my guide and myself, at that hour of the night, he would have taken us for two spectres riding upon nightmares. Will-o'-the-wisps crossed the road from time to time and the jackdaws shrieked fearsomely in the dense woods, where at intervals we saw the gleam of the phosphorescent eyes of wildcats. The manes of the horses tossed more and more wildly, the sweat poured down their sides, and their breath came through their nostrils hard and fast. But when he saw them losing heart, the guide, to encourage them, uttered a guttural cry in which there was nothing human, and they resumed their frenzied course. At last the whirlwind paused; a black mass, with points of light here and there, suddenly reared itself before us; the hoofs of our beasts rang out more loudly upon a strong wooden drawbridge, and we rode beneath an arch which darkly yawned between two enormous towers.

Intense excitement reigned in the palace; servants were crossing the courtyard in all directions, with torches in their hands, and lights ascended and descended from landing to landing. I caught a confused glimpse of huge masses of masonry, of columns, arcades, staircases and balustrades — a riotous luxury of construction, altogether regal and fabulous. A negro page, the same who had handed me Clarimonde's tablets and whom I instantly recognised, assisted me to dismount, and the majordomo, dressed in black velvet, with a gold chain about his neck and an ivory cane in his hand, came forward to meet me. Great tears streamed from his eyes and rolled down his cheeks to his white beard. "Too late!" he cried, shaking his head; "too late, sir priest! But although you have not been able to save the soul, come and keep vigil over the poor body."

He took my arm and led me to the hall

of death; I wept as bitterly as he, for I understood that the dead woman was no other than that Clarimonde whom I had loved so fondly and so madly. A *prie-dieu* was placed beside the bed; a bluish flame, flickering in a bronze patera, cast a wan and deceptive light about the room, and here and there caused some protruding decoration of a piece of furniture or a cornice to twinkle in the darkness. On the table, in a carved vase, was a faded white rose, whose leaves, with the exception of a single one which still clung to the stalk, had all fallen at the foot of the vase, like odorous tears; a broken black masque, a fan, and disguises of all sorts, were lying about on the chairs, and showed that death had appeared in that sumptuous abode unexpectedly and unannounced. I knelt, not daring to turn my eyes towards the bed, and I began to recite the Psalms with great fervour, thanking God that he had placed the grave between the thought of that woman and myself, so that I might

add to my prayers her name, thenceforth
sanctified. But gradually that burst of enthusiasm subsided and I fell into a revery.
That room had nothing of the aspect of a
chamber of death. Instead of the fetid and
cadaverous air which I was accustomed to
breathe in such death-vigils, a languorous
vapour of Oriental essences, an indefinable
amorous odour of woman, floated softly in the
warm air. That pale gleam had rather the
aspect of a subdued light purposely arranged
for purposes of pleasure, than of the yellow
night-light which flickers beside corpses.
I mused upon the strange chance which had
led me to Clarimonde at the very moment
that I lost her forever, and a sigh of regret
escaped from my breast. It seemed to me
that there was an answering sigh behind me,
and I involuntarily turned. It was the echo.
In that movement my eyes fell upon the bed
of death, which they had thus far avoided.
The curtains of red damask with large flowers,
looped back by golden tassels, revealed the

dead woman lying at full length, her hands clasped upon her breast. She was covered with a linen veil of dazzling whiteness, of which the dark purple of the hangings heightened the effect, and of such fineness that it did not at all conceal the charming outlines of her body, and enabled me to follow those lovely lines, as undulating as the neck of a swan, which death itself had not been able to stiffen. She was like an alabaster statue made by some clever sculptor to place upon the tomb of a queen, or like a slumbering maiden upon whom snow had fallen.

I could endure it no longer; that voluptuous atmosphere intoxicated me, that feverish odour of half-withered roses went to my brain, and I paced restlessly back and forth, pausing at every turn beside the platform of the bed to gaze upon the lovely dead woman beneath her transparent winding-sheet. Strange thoughts passed through my mind; I imagined that she was not really dead, and that it was only a feint to which she had resorted to lure me to her palace, and to tell me of her love. For an instant, I even thought that I saw her foot move under the white veil, and disarrange the smooth folds of the shroud.

And then I said to myself: "Is this really Clarimonde? What proof have I of it? May not that black page have entered the service of another woman? I am very foolish to despair thus and to become so excited." But my heart replied with a throb: "It is really she; it is really she." I drew near the bed and gazed with redoubled attention upon the object of my uncertainty. Shall I confess it to you? That perfection of form, although purified and sanctified by the shadow of death, aroused my senses more than it should have done; and that repose was so like sleep that any one might have been deceived. I forgot that I had come there to perform a solemn duty, and I fancied that I was a young bridegroom, entering the bedroom of his betrothed, who conceals her face, from modesty, and refuses to allow him to see her features. Heartbroken with grief, beside myself with joy, quivering with dread and with pleasure, I leaned over her and seized the upper corner of the sheet; I raised it slowly, holding my breath for fear of waking her. My pulses throbbed with such force that I felt the blood hissing through my temples, and my forehead dripped with perspiration, as if I had lifted a marble flagstone. It was in very truth Clarimonde, as I had seen her in the church at the time of my ordination; she was as fascinating as then, and, in her, death seemed but an additional coquetry. The pallor of her cheeks, the less vivid red of her lips, her long lashes, downcast and standing out with their dark fringe against that white flesh, imparted to her face an expression of chaste melancholy and of pensive suffering, whose power of seduction was immeasurable; her long flowing hair, with which were mingled still a few small blue flowers, made a pillow for her head and sheltered with its curls her

The Dead Leman

bare shoulders; her beautiful hands, purer and more transparent than the consecrated wafer, were clasped in an attitude of pious rest and silent prayer, which neutralised what there might have been too alluring, even in death, in the exquisite roundness and ivory polish of her arms, from which the pearl bracelets had not been removed. I stood for a long while absorbed in mute contemplation, and the more I gazed at her, the less I could believe that life had abandoned that lovely body forever. I know not whether it was an illusion or a reflection of the lamp, but one would have said that the blood began to circulate anew beneath that lifeless pallor; however, she continued absolutely motionless. I touched her arm lightly; it was cold, but no colder than her hand on the day that it had touched mine beneath the church porch. I resumed my position, bending my face over hers, and letting the warm dew of my tears rain upon her cheeks. Ah! what a bitter sensation of despair and helplessness!

What a period of agony was that vigil! I would have been glad to be able to collect my life in a pile, in order to give it to her, and to breathe upon her chill remains the flame that consumed me. The night was passing, and realising that the moment of eternal separation was drawing nigh, I could not deny myself the melancholy and supreme pleasure of imprinting a kiss upon the dead lips of her who had had all my love. Oh, miracle! a faint breath mingled with mine, and Clarimonde's lips responded to the pressure of mine; her eyes opened and took on a little life, she heaved a sigh, and unclasping her hands, she put her arms about my neck with an expression of ineffable rapture.

"Ah! is it thou, Romuald?" she said in a voice as languishing and sweet as the dying vibrations of a harp; "what art thou doing, pray? I waited for thee so long that I am dead; but now we are betrothed, and I shall be able to see thee and to come to thee. Adieu, Romuald, adieu! I love thee; that is all that I wished to say to thee, and I give thee back the life to which thou hast recalled me for an instant by thy kiss; we shall soon meet again."

Her head fell back, but she kept her arms about me as if to detain me. A fierce gust of wind blew the window in and entered the room; the last leaf of the white rose fluttered a little longer, like a wing, on the end of the stalk, then became detached and flew away through the open window, carrying with it Clarimonde's soul. The lamp went out, and I fell unconscious on the dead woman's bosom.

When I returned to myself, I was lying in my bed, in my little room at the presbytery, and the former curé's old dog was licking my hand, which lay upon the coverlet. Barbara was bustling about the room with a senile trembling, opening and closing drawers, or stirring powders in glasses. When she saw me open my eyes, the old woman uttered a joyful cry, the dog yelped and wagged his tail; but I was still so weak that I could not utter a single word, nor make a single movement. Afterwards I learned that I had been three days in that condition, giving no other sign of life than an almost imperceptible breathing. Those three days do not count in my life, and I know not where my mind had journeyed during all that time; I have no recollection whatever of it. Barbara told me that the same man with the copper-coloured complexion, who had come to fetch me during the night, had brought me back in the morning in a closed litter and had gone away immediately. As soon as I could collect my thoughts, I reviewed all the incidents of that fatal night. At first I thought that I had been the plaything of some trick of magic; but real and palpable circumstances soon dispelled that theory. I could not believe that I had dreamed, for Barbara had seen as well as I the man with the black horses, whose costume and appearance she described exactly. But no one knew of any castle in the neighbourhood answer-

ing to the description of that where I had
seen Clarimonde.

One morning I saw the Abbé Sérapion enter
my room. Barbara had written him that I
was ill, and he had hastened to me at once.
Although that zeal denoted interest and affec-
tion for my person, his visit did not cause
me the pleasure which it should have done.
There was in the Abbé Sérapion's glance a
penetrating and searching expression which
embarrassed me. I felt ill at ease and guilty
in his presence. He had been the first to
discover my inward distress, and I was
angry with him for his clairvoyance.

While he asked me about my health in a
hypocritically sweet tone, he fixed his yellow
lion-eyes upon me, and plunged his glance
into my very soul, like a sounding-lead. Then
he asked me some questions as to the way in
which I performed my duties, whether I
enjoyed them, how I passed the time which
my ministry left at my disposal, whether I
had made any acquaintances among the

people of the parish, what my favourite books were, and a thousand other similar details. I answered as briefly as possible, and he himself, without waiting for me to finish my answer, passed to another subject. This conversation evidently had no connection with what he desired to say. At last, without any prelude, and as if it were a piece of news which he recalled at the moment and which he was afraid of forgetting, he said to me in a clear and vibrating voice, which rang in my ear like the trumpets of the Last Judgment:

"The famous courtesan Clarimonde died recently, as the result of an orgy which lasted eight days and eight nights. It was something infernally magnificent. They revived the abominations of the feasts of Belshazzar and Cleopatra. Great God! what an age this is in which we live! The guests were served by swarthy slaves speaking an unknown tongue, who to my mind had every appearance of veritable demons; the livery of the meanest among them might have served as a gala-costume for an emperor. There have always been current some very strange stories concerning this Clarimonde, and all her lovers have come to a miserable or a violent end. It has been said that she was a ghoul, a female vampire; but I believe that she was Beelzebub in person."

He ceased to speak and watched me more closely than ever, to see what effect his words had produced upon me. I was unable to refrain from a movement when he mentioned Clarimonde's name, and the news of her death, in addition to the pain that it caused me by reason of its extraordinary coincidence with the nocturnal scene which I had witnessed, produced within me a confusion and a terror which appeared upon my face, strive as I would to control it. Sérapion cast an anxious and stern glance at me; then he said:

"My son, I must warn you that you are standing on the brink of an abyss; beware lest you fall into it. Satan's claws are long, and the grave is not always trustworthy. Clarimonde's tomb should be sealed with a triple seal; for this is not the first time that she has died, so it is said. May God watch over you, Romuald!"

Having said this, Sérapion walked slowly to the door, and I saw him no more; for he returned to S—— almost immediately.

I was entirely restored to health and I had resumed my usual duties. The memory of Clarimonde and the old abbé's words were always present in my mind; but nothing extraordinary had happened to confirm the lugubrious presentiments of Sérapion, and I was beginning to believe that his fears and my own terrors were exaggerated; but one night I had a dream. I had hardly imbibed the first mouthfuls of slumber when I heard the curtains of my bed open and the rings slide upon the rod with a loud noise; I instantly raised myself on my elbow, and I saw a female figure standing before me. I recog-

[218]

nised Clarimonde on the instant. She held in her hand a small lamp of the shape of those which are placed in tombs, and its light imparted to her taper fingers a pink transparence which extended by insensible degrees to the opaque and milky whiteness of her bare arm. Her only clothing was the linen winding-sheet which had covered her upon the bed of death, the folds of which she held about her breast as if ashamed of being so scantily clad; but her little hand did not suffice; she was so white that the colour of the drapery blended with that of the flesh in the pale light of the lamp. Enveloped in that subtle tissue, which revealed the whole contour of her body, she resembled a marble statue of a woman bathing, rather than a real woman endowed with life. Dead or alive, statue or woman, ghost or body, her beauty was still the same: but the green splendour of her eyes was slightly dimmed, and her mouth, formerly so ruddy, was tinted with a faint tender rosiness, almost like that of her cheeks. The little blue flowers which I had noticed in her hair were entirely withered and had lost almost all their petals; all of which did not prevent her from being charming, so charming that, despite the extraordinary character of the adventure, and the inexplicable manner in which she had entered my room, I was not terrified for an instant.

She placed the lamp on the table and seated herself at the foot of my bed; then, leaning towards me, said to me in that voice, at once silvery and soft as velvet, which I have never heard from other lips:

"I have kept thee long in waiting, dear Romuald, and thou mayst well have thought that I had forgotten thee. But I have come from a long distance and from a place from which no one has ever before returned; there is neither moon nor sun in the country from which I come; there is naught but space and shadow; neither road nor path; no ground for the foot, no air for the wing; and yet here I am, for love is stronger than death, and it will end by vanquishing it. Ah! what gloomy faces and what terrible things I have seen in my journeying! What a world of trouble my soul, returned to this earth by the power of my will, has had in finding its body and reinstating itself therein! What mighty efforts I had to put forth before I could raise the stone with which they had covered me! See! the palms of my poor hands are all blistered from it. Kiss them to make them well, dear love! "

She laid the cold palms of her hands on my mouth one after the other; I kissed them again and again, and she watched me with a smile of ineffable pleasure.

To my shame I confess that I had totally forgotten the Abbé Sérapion's warnings and my own priestly character. I fell without resistance and at the first assault. I did not even try to spurn the tempter; the coolness of Clarimonde's flesh penetrated mine, and I felt a voluptuous tremor pass over my whole body.

Poor child! Despite all I have seen, I still

have difficulty in believing that she was a
demon; at all events she had not the aspect
of one, and Satan never concealed his claws
and his horns more deftly. She had drawn
her feet up beneath her, and sat thus on the
edge of my couch, in an attitude full of negli-
gent coquetry. From time to time she passed
her little hand through my hair and twisted
it about her fingers, as if to try the effect of
new methods of arranging my locks about
my face. I allowed her to do it with the
most guilty pleasure, and she accompanied it
all with the most fascinating prattle. It is a
lamentable fact that I felt no astonishment at
such an extraordinary occurrence, and, with
the facility with which one in a dream looks
upon the most unusual events as perfectly
simple, I saw nothing in it all that was not
quite natural.

 ' I loved thee a long while ere I saw thee,
dear Romuald, and I sought thee everywhere. Thou wert my dream, and I spied
thee in the church at the fatal moment. I

said instantly: 'It is he!' I cast a glance at thee, in which I put all the love that I had felt, that I was then feeling, and that I was destined to feel for thee; a glance to lead a cardinal to perdition, to force a king to kneel at my feet before his whole court. Thou didst remain unmoved, and didst prefer thy God to me. Ah! how jealous I am of God, whom thou lovedst and whom thou dost still love better than me! Unhappy woman, unhappy woman that I am! I shall never have thy heart all to myself, I, whom thou didst bring back to life with thy kiss; dead Clarimonde, who for thy sake has forced the doors of the tomb, and who now consecrates to thee a life which she has resumed only to make thee happy!"

All these words were accompanied by maddening caresses which bewildered my senses and my reason to such a point that I did not shrink from uttering a horrible blasphemy to comfort her, and from telling her that I loved her as much as I loved God.

Her eyes recovered their fire and shone like chrysoprases.

"In truth! in very truth? as much as God?" she said, flinging her lovely arms about me. "Since it is so, thou wilt come with me, thou wilt follow me wherever I list. Thou wilt lay aside thy ugly black garments, thou shalt be my lover. To be the acknowledged lover of Clarimonde, who has refused a pope, is magnificent! Ah! what a happy life, what a lovely, golden life we will lead! When shall we start, my fair sir?"

"To-morrow! to-morrow!" I cried in my delirium.

"To-morrow, so be it," she replied. "I shall have time to change my dress, for this is a little scanty and is not suited for travelling. I must also go and notify my servants, who really believe me to be dead and who are as distressed as they can be. Money, clothes, carriages, everything will be ready, and I shall call for thee at this same hour. Adieu, dear heart!"

The Dead Leman

And she lightly touched my forehead with the ends of her lips. The lamp went out, the curtains closed again, and I saw nothing more; a leaden, dreamless sleep fell upon me, and held me unconscious until the morning. I woke later than usual, and the recollection of that strange vision troubled me all day; I ended by persuading myself that it was naught but the vapour of my overheated imagination. And yet the sensation had been so vivid that it was difficult to believe that it was not real; and not without some presentiment of what was about to happen did I retire, after praying God to put away from me evil thoughts and to protect the chastity of my slumber.

I was soon sleeping soundly, and my dream was continued. The curtains were drawn aside and I beheld Clarimonde, not as before, pale in her pale winding-sheet, and with the violet hue of death upon her cheeks, but merry, alert, and smartly dressed, in a magnificent travelling-dress of green velvet, trimmed with gold lace and caught up at the side to reveal a satin petticoat. Her fair hair escaped in huge curls from beneath a broad-brimmed hat of black felt decorated with white feathers capriciously arranged; she held in her hand a little riding-whip with a gold whistle in the handle. She tapped me lightly with it, and said:

"Well! my fine sleeper, is this the way you make your preparations? I expected to find you on your feet. Rise at once, we have no time to lose."

I leaped out of bed.

"Come, dress yourself and let us go," she said, pointing to a small bundle which she had brought; "the horses are impatient and are champing their bits at the door. We should be already ten leagues away."

I dressed myself hastily and she handed me the different parts of my costume, bursting into laughter at my awkwardness, and indicating their respective uses when I made a mistake. She gave a twist to my hair, and when it was done, she handed me a little pocket-mirror of Venetian crystal, with a rim of silver filigree, and said to me:

"How dost find thyself now? Wouldst care to take me into thy service as valet?"

I was no longer the same, and I did not know myself. I resembled myself no more than a finished statue resembles a block of stone. My former face seemed to be only the rough sketch of that which the mirror reflected. I was handsome, and my vanity was sensibly tickled by the metamorphosis. That elegant apparel, that richly embroidered vest, made of me a totally different person, and I marvelled at the power of a few yards of cloth cut in a certain way. The spirit of my costume penetrated my very skin, and within ten minutes I was reasonably conceited.

I walked about the chamber several times to give myself ease of manner. Clarimonde watched me with an air of maternal pleasure, and appeared well satisfied with her work.

"We have had enough of child's play; let

us be off, Romuald dear; we have a long way to go and we shall never arrive."

She took my hand and led me away. All the doors opened before her as soon as she touched them, and we passed by the dog without waking him.

At the gate we found Margheritone; he was the groom who had escorted me before; he was holding three horses, black like the first ones; one for me, one for Clarimonde, and one for himself. Those horses must have been Spanish jennets, born of mares mated with a zephyr; for they went as swiftly as the wind, and the moon, which had risen at our departure to give us light, rolled through the sky like a wheel detached from its carriage; we saw it at our right, jumping from tree to tree, and panting for breath as it ran after us. We soon reached a level tract where, in a clump of trees, a carriage drawn by four beautiful horses awaited us ; we entered it, and the postillions urged them into a mad gallop. I had one arm about Clarimonde's waist and one of her hands clasped in mine; she rested her head on my shoulder, and I felt her bosom, half bare, pressing against my arm. I had never known such bliss. I forgot everything at that moment, and I no more remembered that I had once been a priest than I remembered what I had been doing in my mother's womb, so great was the fascination that the evil spirit exerted upon me. From that night my nature was in a certain sense halved, and there were within me two men, neither of whom knew the other. Sometimes I fancied myself a priest who dreamed every night he was a gentleman, at other times a gentleman who dreamed he was a priest. I could no longer distinguish between dreaming and waking, and I knew not where reality began and illusion ended. The conceited and dissipated young nobleman railed at the priest; the priest loathed the debauchery of the young nobleman. Two spirals entangled in each other and inextricably confounded without ever touching would represent very well the bicephalous life which I led. Despite the abnormality of my position, I do not think that I was mad, for a single instant. I always retained very clearly the consciousness of my two existences. But there was one absurd fact which I could not explain: that was that the consciousness of the same ego could exist in two men so entirely different. It was an anomaly which I did not understand, whether I fancied myself the curé of the little village of C——, or Il Signor Romualdo, the titled lover of Clarimonde.

However, I was, or at least I fancied that I was, at Venice; I have never been able to distinguish between illusion and reality in that extraordinary adventure. We occupied a large marble palace on the Canaleio, filled with frescoes and statues, with two Titians, of the artist's best period, in Clarimonde's bedroom. It was a palace worthy of a king. We had each our gondola and our boatmen in our livery, our music-hall, and our poet. Clarimonde had a magnificent idea of life, and

she had a touch of Cleopatra in her nature.
As for me, I cut the swath of a prince's son,
and I raised such a dust as if I had belonged
to the family of one of the twelve apostles
or of the four evangelists of the Most Serene
Republic; I would not have turned aside from
my path to allow the Doge to pass, and I do
not believe that since Satan fell from heaven,
any creature was ever prouder or more inso-
lent than I. I went to the Ridotto, and I
gambled frantically. I consorted with the
best society in the world, ruined sons of noble
families, actresses, swindlers, parasites, and
swashbucklers; however, despite the dissipated life I led, I remained faithful to Clarimonde. I loved her wildly. She would
have excited satiety itself and chained incon-
stancy. To have Clarimonde was to have
twenty mistresses, she was so mobile, so
changing, and so unlike herself; a very cha-
meleon! She would make you commit with
her the infidelity you might have committed
with others, by assuming the nature, the

manners, and the style of beauty of the woman who seemed to please you. She returned my love a hundredfold; and in vain did young patricians, and even the Ancients of the Council of Ten, make her the most magnificent offers. A Foscari even went so far as to propose to marry her; but she refused everything. She had money enough; she wanted only love, a pure, youthful love, inspired by herself, which should be a first and last passion. I should have been perfectly happy but for an infernal nightmare which recurred every night, and in which I imagined myself a village curé, macerating himself and doing penance for my orgies during the day. Reassured by the habit of being with her, I hardly ever thought of the strange way in which I had made Clarimonde's acquaintance. However, what the Abbé Sérapion had said returned sometimes to my memory and never failed to cause me uneasiness.

For some time Clarimonde's health had become impaired; her bright colour faded from day to day. The doctors whom I summoned failed utterly to understand her disease, and they had no idea what to do. They prescribed some insignificant remedies and came no more. Meanwhile she turned visibly paler, and became colder and colder. She was almost as white and as dead as on that memorable night in the unknown castle. I was in despair to see her thus slowly fall away. She, touched by my grief, would smile at me sweetly and sadly, with the fateful smile of those who feel that they must die.

One morning I was seated by her bed, breakfasting at a small table, in order not to leave her for an instant. As I was cutting some fruit, I accidently made a deep gash in my finger. The blood immediately gushed forth in a purple jet, and a few drops spurted upon Clarimonde. Her eyes flashed and her face assumed an expression of fierce and savage joy which I had never before seen upon it. She jumped out of bed with the agility of a monkey or a cat, and pounced upon my wound, which she began to suck with an expression of unutterable pleasure. She swallowed the blood in little mouthfuls, slowly and gloatingly, as a gourmand sips a wine of Xeres or of Syracuse; she half closed her green eyes, and the lids about them became oblong instead of round. From time to time she paused in order to kiss my hand, then pressed her lips once more to the lips of the wound, to coax forth a few more red drops. When she found that no more blood came, she stood erect with liquid and gleaming eyes, rosier than a May dawn; her face full and fresh, her hand warm and moist,— in fine, lovelier than ever and in the most perfect health.

"I shall not die! I shall not die!" she exclaimed, half mad with joy and clinging to my neck; "I shall be able to love thee for a long time to come. My life is in thine, and all that is of me comes from thee. A few drops of thy rich and noble blood, more precious and more potent than all the elixirs of the world, have restored me to life."

This scene engrossed my thoughts for a long while and aroused within me strange doubts concerning Clarimonde; and that same night, when sleep had taken me back to my presbytery, I saw the Abbé Sérapion, more grave and more anxious than ever. He gazed at me attentively and said:

"Not content with losing your soul, you propose to destroy your body. Wretched young man, into what a snare have you fallen!"

The tone in which he said these few words impressed me deeply; but despite his earnestness, that impression soon vanished and a thousand other preoccupations blotted it from my mind. But one evening I saw in my mirror, the treacherous position of which she had not reckoned upon, Clarimonde pour a powder into the cup of spiced wine which she was accustomed to prepare after our dinner. I took the cup, I pretended to put my lips to it, then placed it upon some piece of furniture, as if to finish it later at my leisure; and taking advantage of a moment when she had her back turned, I tossed the contents under the table; after which I withdrew to my apartment and went to bed, fully determined not to go to sleep and to see what it all meant. I did not wait long; Clarimonde entered in her night-robe, and, having cast it aside, knelt beside my bed. When she was fully assured that I was asleep, she bared my arm and drew a gold pin from her hair; then she murmured in a low voice:

"One drop, just one little red drop, one ruby at the end of my pin! Since thou dost still love me, I must not die. Ah! poor love! I will drink his noble blood, his brilliant purple blood. Sleep, my only treasure, sleep, my god, my child! I will not hurt thee, I will take of thy life only what is necessary to prevent mine from departing. If I did not love thee so dearly I might determine to have other lovers upon whose veins I might draw;

but since I have known thee I have held all the world in horror. Ah! the lovely arm! how round it is! and how white! I shall never dare to prick that pretty blue vein."

And as she said this she wept, and I felt her tears raining upon my arm, as she clasped it in her hands. At last she made up her mind, made a little prick with her pin, and began to suck the blood that flowed from it. Although she had drunk but a few drops, the fear of exhausting me seized her, and she carefully wrapped around my arm a little bandage, afterward rubbing the wound with an unguent which cicatrised it instantly.

I could doubt no longer. The Abbé Sérapion was right. However, despite that certainty, I could not help loving Clarimonde, and I would gladly have given her all the blood that she needed to sustain her factitious life. Besides, I was not much afraid; the woman reassured me concerning the vampire, and what I had heard and seen set my mind at rest; in those days my veins were

richly supplied, and could not be easily exhausted, and I would not haggle for my life
drop by drop. I would have opened my
arm myself and have said to her: "Drink!
and let my love infuse itself into thy body
with my blood!" I carefully avoided making
the slightest allusion to the narcotic which
she had poured out for me, or to the scene
of the pin, and we lived in the most absolute
harmony.

Yet my priestly scruples tormented me
more than ever, and I did not know what
new maceration to invent, to punish and
mortify my flesh. Although all these visions
were involuntary and I had no share in bring-
ing them about, I dared not touch the Christ
with hands so impure, and with a mind
sullied by such debauchery, real or dreamed.
To avoid the recurrence of these fatiguing
hallucinations, I tried to keep from sleeping;
I held my eyelids open with my fingers, and
I stood against the wall, struggling against
sleep with all my might; but the sand of

drowsiness soon entered my eyes, and, seeing that it was useless to struggle, I would drop my arms in discouragement and weariness, and the current would sweep me away towards my perfidious dreams.

Sérapion exhorted me most vehemently, and reproached me severely for my listlessness and my lack of fervour. One day, when I had been more agitated than usual, he said to me:

"To rid you of this obsession, there is but one means, and, although it is an extreme means, we must resort to it; great evils demand heroic remedies. I know where Clarimonde is buried; we must disinter her, so that you may see in what a pitiful plight the object of your love is; you will be tempted no more to imperil your soul for a disgusting corpse, devoured by worms and ready to crumble to dust; that sight will assuredly cause you to reflect."

For my own part, I was so wearied of that double life that I assented, desiring to know

once for all whether the priest or the nobleman was the dupe of a delusion; I was determined to kill, for the benefit of the other,
one of the two men who lived in me, or to
kill them both ; for such a life could not
last.

Abbé Sérapion provided himself with a mattock, a lever, and a lantern, and at midnight
we betook ourselves to the cemetery of——,
of which he knew perfectly the location and
the arrangement.   After turning the light
of the dark lantern upon the inscriptions of
several tombs, we reached at last a stone, half
hidden by tall grass, and devoured by mosses
and parasitic plants, upon which we deci-
phered the opening lines of the epitaph:

> " Here lies Clarimonde
> Who was famed in her lifetime
> As the fairest of women——"

"Here is the place," said Sérapion; and
putting his lantern on the ground, he inserted
the lever in the interstice between the
stones and began to pry.   The stone yielded,

and he set to work with his mattock. For my part, I watched him, more gloomy and silent than the night itself; meanwhile he, bending over his ghastly task, was dripping with perspiration, and his hurried breath was like the rattle of a dying man. It was an extraordinary spectacle, and whoever had seen us from without would have taken us for profane robbers of graves rather than for priests of God. There was something stern and savage in Sérapion's ardour, which made him resemble a demon rather than an apostle or an angel; and his face, with its large, stern features sharply outlined by the light of the lantern, was in no wise reassuring. I felt an icy sweat upon my limbs, and my hair stood painfully erect upon my head; in the inmost depths of my heart, I looked upon the pitiless Sérapion's act as an outrageous sacrilege, and I would have been glad if a triangle of fire had come forth from the dark clouds that moved slowly over our heads and had reduced him to dust. The owls perched upon the cypresses, disturbed by the light of the lantern, beat heavily against the glass with their dusty wings, uttering plaintive cries; wild foxes yelped in the distance, and a thousand sinister noises detached themselves from the silence. At last Sérapion's mattock came in contact with the coffin, the boards of which resounded with a deep, sonorous sound, with that terrible sound nothing utters when stricken. He drew back the lid, and I saw Clarimonde, pale as a marble statue, with clasped hands; her white winding-sheet covered her in a single fold from head to feet. A tiny little drop showed like a rose in the corner of her leaden-hued lips. Sérapion, at that sight, flew into a rage.

"Ah ! there you are, demon, shameless courtesan, drinker of blood and gold!" And he drenched with holy-water the body in the coffin, upon which he made the sign of the cross with his sprinkler. Poor Clarimonde was no sooner touched by the blessed spray than her beautiful body crumbled into dust;

there was nothing left but a ghastly, shapeless mass of cinders and of half-calcined bones.

"Behold your mistress, my Lord Romuald!" cried the inexorable priest, pointing to the sad remains; "shall you be tempted again to promenade on the Lido or at Fusina with your beauty?"

I hung my head; a great catastrophe had taken place within me. I returned to my presbytery, and Lord Romuald, Clarimonde's lover, parted from the poor priest, with whom he had maintained such a strange companionship for so long. But the following night I saw Clarimonde; she said to me as she said the first time, in the church porch: "Unhappy man! Unhappy man! What hast thou done? Why didst thou listen to that foolish priest? Wert thou not happy? And what had I done to thee that thou shouldst violate my poor grave and lay bare the shame of my nothingness? All communication between our souls and our bodies is broken henceforth. Adieu! thou wilt yet regret me."

She vanished in the air like smoke, and I never saw her again.

Alas! she told the truth. I have regretted her more than once, and I regret her still. My soul's peace was purchased very dearly; the love of God was none too much to replace hers. Such, brother, is the story of my youth. Never look upon a woman, and walk abroad always with your eyes on the ground; for, however chaste and watchful you may be, the error of a single moment is enough to cause you to lose eternity.

1836.

The Nest of Nightingales

The Nest of Nightingales

A BOUT the château there was a beautiful park.

In the park there were birds of all kinds; nightingales, blackbirds, and linnets; all the birds of earth had made a rendezvous of the park.

In the spring there was such an uproar that one could not hear one's self talk; every leaf concealed a nest, every tree was an orchestra. All the little feathered musicians vied with one another in melodious contest. Some chirped, others cooed; some performed trills and pearly cadences, others executed bravura passages and elaborate flourishes; genuine musicians could not have done so well.

But in the château there were two fair cousins who sang better than all the birds in the park; Fleurette was the name of one, and Isabeau that of the other. Both were lovely, alluring, and in good case; and on Sundays, when they wore their fine clothes, if their white shoulders had not proved that they were real maidens, one might have taken them for angels; they lacked only wings. When they sang, old Sire de Maulevrier, their uncle, sometimes held their hands, for fear that they might take it into their heads to fly away.

I leave you to imagine the gallant lance-thrusts that were exchanged at tournaments and carrousels in honour of Fleurette and Isabeau. Their reputation for beauty and talent had made the circuit of Europe, and yet they were none the prouder for it; they lived in retirement, seeing almost nobody save the little page Valentin, a pretty, fair-haired child, and Sire de Maulevrier, a hoary-headed old man, all tanned by the sun, and worn out by having borne his war-harness sixty years.

They passed their time in tossing seeds to the little birds, in saying their prayers, and, above all, in studying the works of the masters and in rehearsing together some motet,

The Nest of Nightingales

madrigal, villanelle, or other music of the sort; they also had flowers which they themselves watered and tended. Their life passed in these pleasant and poetical maidenly occupations; they remained in the château, far from the eyes of the world, and yet the world busied itself about them. Neither the nightingale nor the rose can conceal itself; their melody and their perfume always betray them. Now, our two cousins were at once nightingales and roses.

There came dukes and princes to solicit their hands in marriage; the Emperor of Trebizond and the Sultan of Egypt sent ambassadors to propose an alliance to Sire de Maulevrier; the two cousins were not weary of being maidens and would not listen to any mention of the subject. Perhaps a secret instinct had informed them that their mission here on earth was to remain maidens and to sing, and that they would lower themselves by doing anything else.

They had come to that manor when they

were very small. The window of their bedroom looked upon the park, and they had
been lulled to sleep by the singing of the
birds. When they could scarcely walk, old
Blondiau, the old lord's minstrel, had placed
their tiny hands on the ivory keys of the virginal; they had possessed no other toy and
had learned to sing before they had learned to
speak; they sang as others breathed; it was
natural to them.

This sort of education had had a peculiar
influence on their characters. Their melodious childhood had separated them from
the ordinary boisterous and chattering one.
They had never uttered a shriek or a discord-
ant wail; they wept in rhythm and wailed in
tune. The musical sense, developed in them
at the expense of the other senses, made them
quite insusceptible to anything that was not
music. They lived in melodious space, and
had almost no perception of the real world
otherwise than by musical notes. They understood wonderfully the rustling of the foli-

age, the murmur of streams, the striking of the clock, the sigh of the wind in the fireplace, the hum of the spinning-wheel, the dropping of the rain on the shivering grass, all varieties of harmony, without or within; but they did not feel, I am bound to say, great enthusiasm at the sight of a sunset, and they were as little capable of appreciating a painting as if their lovely blue and black eyes had been covered with a thick film. They had the music sickness; they dreamed of it, it deprived them of their appetite; they loved nothing else in the whole world. But, yes, they did love something else—Valentin and their flowers; Valentin because he resembled the roses, the roses because they resembled Valentin. But that love was altogether in the background. To be sure, Valentin was but thirteen years of age. Their greatest pleasure was to sing at their window in the evening the music which they had composed during the day.

The most celebrated masters came from

long distances to hear them and to contend
with them. The visitors had no sooner listened to one measure than they broke their instruments and tore up their scores, confessing
themselves vanquished. In very truth, the
music was so pleasant to the ear and so melodious, that the cherubim from heaven came
to the window with the other musicians, and
learned it by heart to sing to the good Lord.

One evening in May the two cousins were
singing a motet for two voices; never was a
lovelier air more beautifully composed and
executed. A nightingale in the park, perched
upon a rose-bush, listened attentively to them.
When they had finished, he flew to the window, and said to them, in nightingale language:

"I would like to compete in song with
you."

The two cousins replied that they would
do it willingly, and that he might begin.

The nightingale began. He was a master
among nightingales. His little throat swelled,

his wings fluttered, his whole body trembled; he poured forth roulades, flourishes, arpeggios, and chromatic scales; he ascended and descended; he sang notes and trills with discouraging purity; one would have said that his voice, like his body, had wings. He paused, well assured that he had won the victory.

The two cousins performed in their turn; they surpassed themselves. The song of the nightingale, compared with theirs, seemed like the chirping of a sparrow.

The vanquished virtuoso made a last attempt; he sang a love romanza, then he executed a brilliant flourish, which he crowned by a shower of high, vibrating, and shrill notes, beyond the range of any human voice.

The two cousins, undeterred by that wonderful performance, turned the leaves of their book of music, and answered the nightingale in such wise that Saint Cecilia, who listened in heaven, turned pale with jealousy and let her viol fall to earth.

The nightingale tried again to sing, but the contest had utterly exhausted him; his breath failed him, his feathers drooped, his eyes closed, despite his efforts; he was at the point of death.

"You sang better than I," he said to the two cousins, "and my pride, by making me try to surpass you, has cost me my life. I ask one favour at your hands: I have a nest; in that nest there are three little ones; it is on the third eglantine in the broad avenue beside the pond; send some one to fetch them to you, bring them up and teach them to sing as you do, for I am dying."

Having spoken, the nightingale died. The two cousins wept bitterly for him, for he had sung well. They called Valentin, the fair-haired little page, and told him where the nest was. Valentin, who was a shrewd little rascal, readily found the place; he put the nest in his breast and carried it to the château without harm. Fleurette and Isabeau, leaning on the balcony rail, were awaiting him impatiently. Valentin soon arrived, holding the nest in his hands. The three little ones had their heads over the edge, with their beaks wide open. The girls were moved to pity by the little orphans, and fed them each in turn. When they had grown a little they began their musical education, as they had promised the vanquished nightingale.

It was wonderful to see how tame they became, how well they sang. They went fluttering about the room, and perched now upon Isabeau's head, now upon Fleurette's shoulder. They lighted in front of the music-book, and in very truth one would have said that they were able to read the notes, with such an intelligent air did they scan the white ones and the black ones. They learned all Fleurette's and Isabeau's melodies, and began to improvise some very pretty ones themselves.

The two cousins lived more and more in solitude, and at night strains of supernal melody were heard to issue from their chamber. The nightingales, perfectly taught, took their parts in the concert, and they sang almost as well as their mistresses, who themselves had made great progress.

Their voices assumed each day extraordinary brilliancy, and vibrated in metallic and crystalline tones far above the register of the natural voice. The young women grew perceptibly thin; their lovely colouring faded; they became as pale as agates and almost as transparent. Sire de Maulevrier tried to prevent their singing, but he could not prevail upon them.

As soon as they had sung a measure or two, a little red spot appeared upon their cheek-bones, and grew larger and larger until they had finished; then the spot disappeared, but a cold sweat issued from their skin, and their lips trembled as if they had a fever.

But their singing was more beautiful than ever; there was in it a something not of this world, and to one who heard those sonorous and powerful voices issuing from those two fragile maidens, it was not difficult to foresee what would happen—that the music would shatter the instrument.

They realised it themselves, and returned to their virginal, which they had abandoned for vocal music. But one night, the window was open, the birds were twittering in the park, the night wind sighed harmoniously; there was so much music in the air that they could not resist the temptation to sing a duet which they had composed the night before.

It was the *Swan's Song*, a wondrous melody all drenched with tears, ascending to the most inaccessible heights of the scale, and redescending the ladder of notes to the lowest round; something dazzling and incredible; a deluge of trills, a fiery rain of chromatic flourishes, a display of musical fireworks impossible to describe; but meanwhile the little red spot grew rapidly larger and almost covered their cheeks. The three nightingales watched them and listened to them with painful anxiety; they flapped their wings, they went and came and could not remain in one place. At

last the maidens reached the last bar of the
duet; their voices assumed a sonority so extraordinary that it was easy to understand
that they who sang were no longer living
creatures. The nightingales had taken flight.
The two cousins were dead; their souls had
departed with the last note. The nightingales had ascended straight to heaven to
carry that last song to the good Lord, who
kept them all in His Paradise, to perform the
music of the two cousins for Him.

Later, with these three nightingales, the
good Lord made the souls of Palestrina, of
Cimarosa, and of Gluck.

1833.

Poems

Poems

*L*OVE at *Sea* is published in this volume by the permission of Algernon Charles Swinburne; *Ars Victrix*, by permission of Austin Dobson, and by the authorisation of Dodd, Mead & Co., the holders of the American copyright. *The Cloud, The Portal,* and *The Chimera* are here used by special arrangement with George D. Sproul (copyright, 1903), and are taken from his edition in English of the works of Théophile Gautier, edited by F.-C. de Sumichrast. *The Yellow Stains* is here used by permission of Brentano's, its publishers, and is taken from their volume, *One of Cleopatra's Nights,* translated from the French of Gautier by Lafcadio Hearn.

The Poet and the Crowd, The Caravan, The Marsh, and *Earth and the Seasons* were especially translated for this volume, and are covered by the general copyright. The names appended to the poems are those of the translators.

[261]

LOVE AT SEA

WE are in love's land to-day;
  Where shall we go?
Love, shall we start or stay,
  Or sail or row?
There's many a wind and way,
And never a May but May;
We are in love's hand to-day;
  Where shall we go?

Our land-wind is the breath
Of sorrows kiss'd to death
  And joys that were;
Our ballast is a rose;
Our way lies where God knows
  And love knows where.
    We are in love's hand to-day—

Our seamen are fledged Loves,
Our masts are bills of doves,

Théophile Gautier

Our decks fine gold;
Our ropes are dead maids' hair,
Our stores are love-shafts fair
   And manifold.
      We are in love's land to-day—

Where shall we land you, sweet?
On fields of strange men's feet,
   Or fields near home?
Or where the fire-flowers blow,
Or where the flowers of snow
   Or flowers of foam?
      We are in love's hand to-day—

Land me, she says, where love
Shows but one shaft, one dove,
   One heart, one hand,—
A shore like that, my dear,
Lies where no man will steer,
   No maiden land.
      Algernon Charles Swinburne.

Ars Victrix

ARS VICTRIX

Yes; when the ways oppose —
  When the hard means rebel,
Fairer the work out-grows, —
  More potent far the spell.

O Poet, then, forbear
  The loosely-sandalled verse,
Choose rather thou to wear
  The buskin — strait and terse;

Leave to the tiro's hand
  The limp and shapeless style;
See that thy form demand
  The labour of the file.

Sculptor, do thou discard
  The yielding clay, — consign
To Paros marble hard
  The beauty of thy line; —

[265]

Théophile Gautier

Model thy Satyr's face
    For bronze of Syracuse;
In the veined agate trace
    The profile of thy Muse.

Painter, that still must mix
    But transient tints anew,
Thou in the furnace fix
    The firm enamel's hue;

Let the smooth tile receive
    Thy dove-drawn Erycine;
Thy Sirens blue at eve
    Coiled in a wash of wine.

All passes.   Art alone
    Enduring stays to us;
The Bust outlasts the throne,—
    The Coin, Tiberius;

Even the gods must go;
    Only the lofty Rhyme
Not countless years o'erthrow,—
    Not long array of time.

Ars Victrix

Paint, chisel, then, or write;
  But, that the work surpass,
With the hard fashion fight,—
  With the resisting mass.

Austin Dobson.

THE CLOUD

LIGHTLY in the azure air
Soars a cloud, emerging free
Like a virgin from the fair
  Blue sea;

Or an Aphrodite sweet,
Floating upright and impearled
In the shell, about its feet
  Foam-curled.

Undulating overhead,
How its changing body glows!
On its shoulder dawn hath spread
  A rose.

Marble, snow, blend amorously
In that form by sunlight kissed —
Slumbering Antiope
  Of mist!

The Cloud

Sailing unto distant goal,
Over Alps and Apennines,
Sister of the woman-soul,
    It shines;

Till my heart flies forth at last
On the wings of passion warm,
And I yearn to gather fast
    Its form.

Reason saith: " Mere vapour thing!
Bursting bubble!   Yet, we deem,
Holds this wind-distorted ring
    Our dream."

Faith declareth: "Beauty seen,
Like a cloud, is but a thought,
Or a breath, that, having been,
    Is naught.

"Have thy vision.   Build it proud.
Let thy soul be full thereof.
Love a woman — love a cloud —
    But love!"

                 Agnes Lee.

Théophile Gautier

THE POET AND THE CROWD

THE plain reproached the idle mountain:
    "Naught
  Can ever grow on thy wind-beaten brow!"
The poet, bending o'er his lyre in thought,
  Heard the Crowd say: "Dreamer, what use
    art thou?"

In anger spoke the mountain to the plain:
    "'T is I that make thy harvests sprout and
    grow!
I cool the South's hot breath, I send the rain,
  I stay the clouds in Heaven, or bid them go.

"I mould the avalanches in my hand,
  I melt in crucibles the crystal gleams
Of glaciers; from my breasts o'er all the land
  I pour abroad the bright life-giving streams."

The Poet and the Crowd

Even so the poet to the Crowd replied:
　"Suffer me thus to rest my pallid brow.
Hath not my very soul poured from my side
　For fountain where the race are drinking
　　now?"

Curtis Hidden Page.

Théophile Gautier

THE PORTAL

O ARTIST, man, whoever thou mayst be,
Marvel not through so sad a gate to see
This new-born volume fatally unfold!

Alas! all monument built high, complete,
Before it raise its head must plunge its feet:
The skyward tower hath felt the secret mould.

Below, the night-bird and the tomb.   Above,
Rose of the sun and whiteness of the dove,
Carols and bells on every arch of gold.

Above, the minarets, the window's charm,
Where birdlings fret their wings in sunbeams
     warm,—
The carved escutcheons borne by angels tall,

Acanthus leaves and lotus flowers of stone,
Like lilies in Elysian gardens blown.
Below, rude shaft and vault elliptical,

The Portal

Knights rigid on their biers the deathlong days,
With folded hands and helpless upward gaze,
And from the cavern roofs the drips that fall.

My book is builded thus, with narrow line
Of stratum stone, embossed with many a sign,
And carven words the creeping mosses fill.

God grant that, passing o'er this humble place,
The pilgrim foot shall never quite efface
Its poor inscription and its work's unskill.

My ghostly dead! That ye might walk the
    shades,
With patience have I wrought your colon-
    nades,
And in my Campo Santo couched you still.

There watcheth at your side an angel true,
To make a curtain of his wing for you,
Pillow of marble, cloth of leaden fold.

Théophile Gautier

Yea, Righteousness and Peace have kissed in
    stone,
Mercy and Truth are met together, one
In flowing raiment, fair and aureoled.

A sculptured greyhound lieth at your heels.
A beauteous child eternally appeals
From out the shadow of the tomb enscrolled.

Upon the pillars arabesques arise
Of blooming vines that flutter circlewise,
As o'er espalier twines the dappled green.

And the dark tomb appears a gladsome thing,
With all this bright, perpetual flowering,
And looks on sorrow with a smile serene.

Death plays coquette.   Only her forehead fair
Hath pallor still beneath her ebon hair.
She seeks to charm, and hath a royal mien.

A burst of colour fires the blazons clear;
The alabaster melts to whitest tear;
Less hard uplooms the bronze-built sepulture.

The Portal

The consorts lie upon their beds of state;
Their pillows seem to soften with their
    weight,
Their love to flower within the marble pure;

Till with her garlands, traceries, and festoons,
Trefoils, pendentives, pillars wrought with
    runes,
Fantasia at her will may laugh and lure.

The tomb becomes a thing of bright parade,
A throne, a holy altar, an estrade,
For it is wish fulfilled of sight at last.

But if, by some capricious thought impelled,
Your hand should peradventure wonder-
    spelled   · · ·
Upraise a cover rich with carven cast,

Under the heavy vault and architrave,
You still would find within the mouldering
    grave
The stiff and white cadaver sheeted fast,

Théophile Gautier

With never glimmer of a ray without,
Nor inner light to flood the bier about,
As in the pictures of the Holy Tomb.

Between her thin arms, like a tender spouse
Death binds her chosen to her, nor shall rouse
Them ever, nor let go her grasp of doom.

Scarce at the Judgment Hour their heads shall
    stir,
When at the trumpet blast the stars shall err,
And a strange wind blow out the torch's
    plume.

An angel shall discern them in his quest,
Upon the ruins of the world at rest,
For they shall sleep and sleep, the cycles long.

And if the Christ Himself should raise His
    hand,
As unto Lazarus, to bid them stand,
The grave would loosen not its fetter strong.

The Portal

A tomb enwrought with sculpture is my verse,
That hides a body under leaf and thyrse,
And breaks its weeping heart to seem a song.

My poems are graves of mine illusions dead,
Where many a wild and luckless form I bed
When a ship founders in the tempest's peal!—

Abortive dream, ambition's eagerness,
All secret ardours, passions issueless,—
All bitter, intimate things that life can feel.

Each day the sea devours a goodly ship.
Close to the shore there hides a reef to rip
Her copper-sheathèd flanks and iron keel.

How many have I launched, with what fair
names!
With silken streamers coloured like the
flames,—
Never to cleave the harbour sun's reflex!

Ah, what dear passengers, what faces sweet,—
Desires with heaving breasts, hopes, visions
fleet,—
O my heart's children swarming to the decks!

Théophile Gautier

The sea hath shrouded them with glaucous
    taint:
The red of rose, the alabaster faint,
The star, the flower, lie floating in the wrecks.

Fearful and masterful, the hurtling tide
Dashes from drifting spar to dolphin side
My stark and drownèd dreams that sink and
    part.

For these inglorious travellers distant-bound,
Pale seekers of Americas unfound,
Curve into hollow caverns, O mine Art!

Then rise in towers and cupolas of fire,
Press upward in a bold cathedral spire,
And fix your peak in heaven's open heart!

Ye little birds of love and fantasy,
Sonnets, white birds of heaven's poetry,
Light softly on my gables argentine.

And swallows, April messengers that pass,
Beat not your tender wings against the glass,—
My marbles have their rifts where you may win.

The Portal

My virgin saint shall hide you in her robe,
For you the emperor shall let fall his globe,
The lotus heart spread wide to nest you in.

I 've reared mine azure arch, mine organ
      grand,
I 've carved my pillars, placed with loving
      hand
In each recess a saint of martyrdom:

I 've begged a chalice of Elygius,—spice
And frankincense for holy sacrifice
Of Kaspar, and have drawn the sweet there-
      from.

The people kneel at prayer.   The radiant
      priest
In orphreyed chasuble prepares the Feast.
The church is builded, Lord!   Then wilt Thou
      come ?

                              Agnes Lee.

Théophile Gautier

THE CARAVAN

The human caravan day after day
    Along the trail of unreturning years,
    Parched with the heat, and drinking sweat
        and tears,
Across the world's Sahara drags its way.

Great lions roar, and muttering storms dismay.
    Horizons flee, no spire nor tower appears,
    Nor shade, save when the vulture's shadow
        nears,
Crossing the sky to seek his filthy prey.

Still onward and still onward, till at last
    We see a place of greenness cool and blest,
        Strewn with white stones, where cy-
        press-shade lies deep.

Oasis-like, along Time's desert waste,
    God sets His burial-grounds, to give you rest.
        Ye way-spent travellers, lie down, and
        sleep.
                  Curtis Hidden Page.

THE MARSH

Iᴛ is a marsh, whose sleepy water
Lies stagnant, covered with a mantle
Of lily-pads and rushes;
And at the least noise, the croaking frogs
Dive under their light-green cover.
To it flies the black and gray snipe
When, on a frosty November morning,
The bleak north wind blows;
Often, from the dark clouds above,
Plover, lapwing, curlew, and crane
Alight there, weary from a long flight.
Under the creeping duck-weed
The wild ducks dip
Their sapphire necks glazed with gold;
At dawn the teal is seen bathing,
And when twilight reigns,
It settles between two rushes and sleeps.
The stork that snaps his bill,
With eye turned towards the opaque sky,

Théophile Gautier

Awaits there the time of departure;
And the heron with slender legs,
Smoothing the feathers of its wings,
Drags out there its lonely life.
Friend, when the autumnal mist
Spreads its uniform mantle
Over the gloomy face of heaven,
When the whole town is slumbering
And when the day is just breaking
On the silent horizon,
You whose shot always carries
Sure death to the swallow,
You who, at thirty paces,
Ne'er missed the fleet-footed hare,
Friend, indefatigable hunter,
Not to be deterred by a long journey,
With Rasko, your dog that follows,
Bounding behind through the high grass,
With your good bronzed gun,
Your hunting-jacket, and your whole outfit,
Go and hide there near the bank,
Behind the trunk of a broken tree.
Your sport will be deadly;

The Marsh

Through the meshes of your game-bag
Many a bird's legs will pass.
And you will return early,
Reaching home at dusk
With joyful heart and kindled eyes.

Robert Louis Sanderson.

EARTH AND THE SEASONS

THE rose-pink Earth in April wears
    The flush of youth;
A maiden still, she hardly dares
    To meet Spring's troth!

When June comes, paler grows her brow
    In passion's pain.
She hides with sunburnt Summer now
    Among the grain.

In August's mad bacchante mood
    She bares her breast
To Autumn, rolling in the blood
    Of grapes new-pressed.

And in December, weazened, old,
    Frost-powdered, white,
She dreams beside old Winter cold,
    Who sleeps all night.

                Curtis Hidden Page.

The Yellow Stains

THE YELLOW STAINS

WITH elbow buried in the downy pillow
      I 've lain and read,
All through the night, a volume strangely
    written
      In tongues long dead.

For at my bedside lie no dainty slippers;
      And, save my own,
Under the paling lamp I hear no breathing:—
      I am alone!

But there are yellow bruises on my body
      And violet stains;
Though no white vampire came with lips
    blood-crimsoned
      To suck my veins!

Now I bethink me of a sweet, weird story
      That in the dark
Our dead loves thus with seal of chilly kisses
      Our bodies mark.

Théophile Gautier

Gliding beneath the coverings of our couches
       They share our rest,
And with their dead lips sign their loving
      visit
          On arm and breast.

Darksome and cold the bed where now she
      slumbers,
         I loved in vain,
With sweet, soft eyelids closed, to be reopened
         Never again.

Dead sweetheart, can it be that thou hast lifted
        With thy frail hand
Thy coffin-lid, to come to me again
        From Shadowland ?

Thou who, one joyous night, didst, pale and
      speechless,
        Pass from us all,
Dropping thy silken mask and gift of flowers
        Amidst the ball ?

The Yellow Stains

Oh, fondest of my loves, from that far heaven
    Where thou must be,
Hast thou returned to pay the debt of kisses
    Thou owest me?

Lafcadio Hearn.

Théophile Gautier

THE CHIMERA

A YOUNG chimera at my goblet's brim
   Gave sweetest kiss amid the orgy's spell.
Emerald her eyes, and to her haunches slim
   The golden torrent of her tresses fell.

Her shoulders fluttering pinions did bedeck.
   I sprang upon her back, for travel fain,
And toward me bending firm her lovely neck,
   I plunged my tightening fingers in her mane.

She struggled madly; but I clung, austere;
   With iron knees I crushed her flanks to me.
Then softly came her voice, and silver-clear:
   "Whither, then, master, shall I carry thee?"

To farthest edge of all eternal things,
   Beyond the sun, beyond the bounds of space;
But weary ere the end shall be thy wings,—
   For I would see my vision face to face.
                Agnes Lee.